Name Your Mountain

Tim Tingle

Library of Congress Cataloging-in-Publication Data available upon request.

7th Generation
an imprint of Book Publishing Company
PO Box 99, Summertown, TN 38483
888-260-8458
bookpubco.com
nativevoicesbooks.com

ISBN: 978-1-939053-20-6

25 24 23 22 21 20   1 2 3 4 5 6 7 8 9

Contents

Dedicated to the South Houston
High School Class of 1967.

The older we become,
the closer we grow.

CHAPTER 1

Summertime at the Court

"Can we ever have a single day of our lives without trouble?" I asked.

Dad glanced at me, then turned his attention to the road without speaking. I stared out the window as we drove by the hospital.

"We've been there plenty of times," I said.

"I've been there more than you, Bobby," Dad said. "At least one more day than you. I drove your mom to the hospital on a Monday and you were born the next morning. So, my son, because of you I had to spend the night in the hospital."

"Was it worth it?" I asked.

"The jury's still out on that one," Dad said.

"Dad! I am your firstborn, your only child. How can you say that?"

Dad pulled into the parking lot of the city park, near the basketball court. He had a cool, fatherly smile on his face, and I slapped my palm against his shoulder. Choctaws let friends and family know they love them in many ways, and jokes and comebacks and shoulder slaps were common.

"Did you bring the mop and bucket?" I asked.

Dad tilted his head and gave me his favorite *Where is this going?* look.

"Oh, sorry, Dad," I said. "I almost forgot. I'm the son that's gonna mop you up. Right?"

"That'll be the day," Dad said. He opened the back door and grabbed our shoes and basketball. We both hurried to a bench, tossed our everyday shoes aside, put on our b-ball sneakers, and stepped onto the court.

For my father and me, stepping onto the basketball court was like entering another universe. Worries of the "real world" were put aside. We had both spent much of our lives working and practicing and driving ourselves to a new place in life—we were basketball players who played tough and hard, but fair.

"And nobody gets hurt," as Coach Robison always said.

For years, during my dad's drinking days, he always came home from work mad about something. He never knew I played basketball. He never worried about where I was every afternoon. I was here, dribbling and shooting.

I was here to get away from my father, the cool and friendly man I now called Dad. I was here to keep from being shoved and pushed aside and cussed out. I was here, on the basketball court, to keep from being hurt.

I am convinced that Dad always cared for me, even loved me. But he didn't know how to show it, and he was afraid of me as much as I was afraid of him.

And why? What could I do to hurt him?

I made him feel guilty, that's what I did. He knew that drinking and breaking furniture and shoving people was wrong. And he finally quit drinking and became the coolest father ever.

And why?

Because I drove my friend's car into Lake Thunderbird in the middle of the night and almost drowned. As Dad and Mom stood by my bedside, with my life seeping away, Dad leaned over to Mom. He didn't know I could hear him, but I could.

"If Bobby comes back to us, I will never have another drink for the rest of my life. I promise."

I squeezed his hand. I couldn't speak, but I let him know I was still alive and going to survive. Our lives were changed forever.

Since I spent so much time here at the basketball court growing up, I became a pretty good player. I'm not bragging, *I'm just saying*. I learned to dribble with both hands. I could keep my pivot foot down and fake hard to the right, and when my defender jumped to stop me, I simply drove to my left and left him behind.

But since I'm a guard, a playmaker, and a shooter, I am not tall enough to roam around the basket all day. No, my favorite shot will always be the three-pointer, the long shot. When I was a kid, in the fourth or fifth grade, I let fly from maybe twenty feet away, and I sometimes hit the bottom of the net. But now, as a soon-to-be junior in high school, I have a sweet jump shot.

I often fake left or right, to keep my defender on the ground, then leap high and let fly with a high-arching jumper. *Nothing but net!* Hopefully.

Back to today.

"Hoke, Dad, let me know when you're ready for some one-on-one," I said.

"I'm an old man," Dad said. "I need to stretch my tired old muscles and warm up first. I need to take a few practice shots." Dad took a deep breath, puffed his chest, and waved his arms in wide circles—first one, then the other. "All right, I'll give it a try."

I rolled the ball across the concrete court. Dad picked it up, then closed his eyes prayerfully. When he opened them, he took a few dribbles and stepped back, almost to the grass.

"Careful not to fall off the court, Dad," I shouted.

He stared at the basket, then launched a long, high shot from the far corner. It sailed high over the treetops and soon settled in the bottom of the net.

"Not bad, Dad," I said. "But I bet you can't make another one."

"Bobby, show your old dad some respect," he said. "But I'll take you on. You say you bet I can't make another shot? Is that right?"

"You heard me, Dad."

"If we're making a bet, what's the gamble?" he asked.

I didn't hesitate. Maybe, just maybe, my dream will come true.

"Hoke, how about this, Dad. If you miss your next shot, you buy me a new car for Christmas. This year."

"And if I make it, you buy your own car?" Dad asked.

How could I not take the risk? A new car for Christmas!

"You're on, Dad," I said as I slowly rolled the ball to him.

What happened next was *so much my dad*.

He didn't take another three-pointer. No, he took a few dribbles, drove to the basket, and sank a layup.

"That's not fair!" I shouted. "Dad, you were supposed to make a long shot from the corner."

"Son, if you're making a bet, you better pay attention to what you say. You bet me

I couldn't *make another shot*, you didn't say where from."

I closed my eyes, hung my head, and smiled. How can you not love this man?

I knew he'd help me get a car when he thought I was ready. But he won the gamble.

CHAPTER 2

The Real Fun Begins

Dad and I stayed at the park for at least an hour, shooting and rebounding, tossing the ball back and forth. We played a few games of one-on-one, with Dad using his height to back up to the basket and shoot over me. And I used my quickness to drive around him, sometimes ducking under the basket to score with my left hand. Dad was never so proud of me as when I scored with my left hand, so I did it for him.

When I saw him sweating and breathing hard, I knew it was almost time to go.

"How about some free throws, Dad?" I asked.

"Sure thing, Bobby. Best out of ten and you go first?"

I stood at the free-throw line, took my usual four dribbles, and made my first seven shots. When I finally missed number eight, I slapped my forehead. "I thought I had it," I said.

I did make the next two shots, and Dad said, "Well, Bobby, nine out of ten free throws isn't that bad." He took the ball, walked to the line, and made his first five shots.

"You're gonna make all ten free throws, Dad. I know it," I said.

"You're trying to jinx me, aren't you, Bobby?"

I smiled and shrugged my shoulders.

Dad nodded, took the ball, and walked toward the car.

"Hey, where are you going?" I called out.

"Home, Bobby. And I won. You made ninety percent of your free throws and I made one hundred percent. Nice try, son."

As we pulled away from the park, I patted Dad on the shoulder. "I'm still proud to have you as my dad."

"Same here, Bobby," Dad replied. "Big time."

We pulled into the driveway, and Mom met us at the front door with a welcoming smile. "Coach Robison called looking for you," she said.

"I guess I left my phone in the car," Dad said, "and I didn't check for messages."

"He was concentrating on free throws, Mom," I said, "and he made one hundred percent."

"What did he want?" Dad asked.

"He wanted to update you on Mr. Mackey," Mom said.

Mr. Mackey was a lawyer and Johnny's dad. Johnny was Cherokee, my best friend, and a center on our basketball team. Just this morning, while replacing shingles on his roof, Mr. Mackey fell off the ladder. He couldn't move, and Mrs. Mackey called for an ambulance. He was rushed to the hospital with a possible broken hip.

"How's he doing?"

"His hip isn't broken, but he'll be in a wheelchair for a while. At least that's how it looks now," Mom said.

Dad turned to me with raised eyebrows. "Bobby," he said, "if you ever graduate from law school and have a very successful practice, promise me you won't climb on the roof of your house to replace rotten shingles."

"Hoke, Dad," I said. "If I graduate from law school, which I have no interest in attending, then I will never replace my own shingles. I promise."

Dad turned to Mom. "Will he be there overnight?" he asked.

"No, he should be home in a few hours."

"Then we won't bother him," said Dad. "They have enough to worry about."

"I'll give Johnny a call," I said, and I stepped to the backyard with my phone.

Johnny answered the phone on the first ring.

"What's up?' he said.

"I just want to know how you're doing. And how's the old man?"

"I guess you've heard," Johnny said. "Why he didn't call our roof repairman I'll never know."

"You already know, Johnny," I said. "Your dad still sees himself as a hardworking man, not above the working class. Just like mine."

"Yeah, I know, and I guess I should be proud of him for that."

"You're still coming to practice tomorrow?"

"Of course I'm coming to practice," Johnny said. "Ten o'clock sharp. Things are getting pretty serious now. I just hope we're good enough to stay on the court with these guys."

I had the same doubts and fears as Johnny, but with his dad in the hospital, I wanted to stay positive. And why be afraid of a loss? In the first place, we almost never lose a basketball game. We are a team of Native American All-Stars—the Achukmas—from across the state of Oklahoma, and we are playing in a national summer league tournament. We have already clinched our regional title, winning the final game after a crazy weekend of having two of our best players sent to jail.

On the night before the finals, they were accused of robbing a late-night convenience store, and of course they were innocent. And who were the real robbers, wearing our team's basketball jerseys and masks? Ballplayers from the team we were facing in the semifinals! But that's over. We won, so we're off to the next battle—which always includes more than basketball.

"We've come this far, Johnny," I said. "Coach will keep it close and the rest is up to us. I'm thinking we can stay with anybody."

"So far, so good," Johnny said. "Say, can I come over for a while?"

"Only if you want some of Mom's cherry pie, served warm with scoops of vanilla ice cream on top."

"I'm on my way," Johnny said.

I hung up and strolled to the kitchen.

"Hey, Mom! Johnny's coming over. He's really worried about his dad, and I thought your cherry pie, topped with ice cream, would make him feel better."

"And while I'm at it, I should warm some up for you and your dad. Is that right, Bobby?" Mom asked.

"Gee, I never thought of that. But yeah, now that you mention it, I guess I'd like some too. How about you, Dad?"

Ten minutes later Johnny arrived, giving Mom plenty of time to have our afternoon desserts already on the patio picnic table, along with tall glasses of raspberry lemonade. Dad and Mom left us alone to visit. Looking back on our conversation, I was glad they did.

As he chewed and swallowed his first piece of cherry pie, Johnny gave me a long and serious look. "Did your mom tell you the police stopped by the house?" he asked.

"The police! No, she didn't say anything about that. Why? What's going on?"

Johnny kept his eyes on me as he took a drink of lemonade.

"Hoke, I get it," I said. "Mum's the word. I won't say anything to anybody."

"Good," Johnny said, taking a deep breath. "You know Dad has prosecuted some serious criminal cases?"

I nodded but kept quiet.

"He has lots of enemies, both in and out of prison," Johnny said. "The police are investigating. They think Dad's fall was no accident."

"How can that be, Johnny?"

"I know it sounds crazy," Johnny said. "But you know how my dad is. Total attention to detail. He's that way about everything. There's no way he would climb to the roof of our house on a broken ladder. He inspects every tool before using it."

"A broken ladder?" I asked. "What do you mean?"

Johnny took another swig of lemonade before replying.

"It was a new ladder, and Dad had already climbed it the evening before his fall. No problems. But the next morning, when he climbed to the roof, the top rung of the ladder broke off. That's when Dad fell to the ground and almost broke his hip."

"How could that happen?"

"While Dad was lying on the ground, in terrible pain, he saw that the screws on the top rung of the ladder were loose. Somebody had taken a screwdriver to 'em."

"Do they have any idea who?" I asked.

"They have a few suspects. A few men that Dad convicted and sent to jail are out now, and they live in the area."

"Wow. I don't know what to say, Johnny."

"And I don't know what to do. We've always thought of this as the safest neighborhood in the world," Johnny said. "But if the police are right, if somebody is out to hurt my dad, none of us are safe."

"This reminds me of why I dug my backyard hole," I said.

"Yeah," said Johnny with a smile. "But I don't think your hole is big enough for my entire family." I saw tears forming in his eyes, and I gave him a strong brother-hug.

"I'm here for you, Johnny," I said. "Always."

"I know," he said, "and that means a lot."

Johnny and I said nothing for a long while. We finished our cherry pie and washed it down with ice-cold lemonade. Finally, I gave him a look that said, *So, what are you going to do?*

"Dad has to be agonizing," Johnny said, sliding his plate away and leaning back in his chair. "He considers all options, even the worst. That's what a lawyer has to do. I'm sure he and Mom have talked about it, but they're not saying a thing to me."

"Johnny," I said with a slight smile, "you're a lot like your dad. Where is your mind going?"

"Here's what we cannot avoid," he said. "If Dad is in danger from someone he sent to jail…"

"Or even a friend of someone he sent to jail," I interrupted.

"Yes, I've thought of that too. And here's the worst of it. If Dad is in danger, then so is Mom."

"And so are you," I said, then wished I hadn't.

Johnny took a long deep breath, looked to the sky, and gripped his hands behind his head. "What I have told you goes nowhere," he said. "And what I am about to say must stay between us."

"Big-time promise," I replied.

"I don't know if I'll ever play basketball again. I was lying when I said I'll be at practice tomorrow."

"Johnny! This has nothing to do with you, or basketball!"

Johnny said nothing. He looked at me and waited, lifting his eyebrows and tilting his head.

"You're thinking that you are not safe here anymore, is that it?" I asked.

"Exactly," Johnny said, "and if I came to that conclusion, so did Dad. The last time I was at the hospital, the police dropped by and Dad asked me to leave the room."

"Any idea what they said?" I asked.

"I know exactly what they said," he replied. "The room next door to Dad's was empty. There were no nurses in the hallway, so I slipped in. There was a door between the two rooms, and I put my ear to the door."

"Sounds like your lawyer dad raised a detective son," I said.

Johnny gave me a brief smile and nodded. Troubled times need a touch of humor.

"Dad had apparently called the police on the way to the hospital. He asked them to check the backyard and the patio for any unusual footprints, any sign that someone had climbed over the fence the night before he fell."

"The night before?" I asked.

"Yes," Johnny said. "Dad left the ladder leaning against the house when he finished working on the roof. He knew he'd get started early Saturday morning. That's my dad. He was up before breakfast."

"That's my dad, too," I said. "He'd be on the roof before the sun rose."

"Well," Johnny said, looking down, "Dad never made it to the roof."

"And your lives will never be the same," I said.

Johnny nodded.

"But, Johnny," I said, "you know what Coach Robison will say."

"There's always a way," said Johnny. "I can hear him saying it now."

"There's always a way," I replied. "Play hard, play tough, and nobody gets hurt. And Johnny, the struggle won't be easy, but you won't get hurt. And neither will anyone in your family."

"And how do you know that?" Johnny asked.

I shrugged my shoulders, looked to the sky, and smiled.

CHAPTER 3

Home to the Underground

We sipped our lemonade in silence, but not for long.

"Hey! What's all the talk about?"

We looked up, and my next-door neighbor, Faye—or my girlfriend, Faye, depending on who you're talking to—stood in the backyard.

"Faye, how did you get here?" I asked, waving my palms in the air.

Faye pointed to my backyard underground room, my getaway. The roof was a door covered with branches and weeds, so it seemed part of the unmowed yard. I had dug a big hole and made it my underground room to get away from Dad, back when he was still drinking. Now it was a place to gather with friends for serious talks or just to get away—complete with microwave and refrigerator!

Faye had quietly climbed into the room while we sat on the back patio. She had heard everything!

"I'm not liking this," Johnny said.

"If you're afraid I heard about your dad and the ladder, and your family being in danger, I did," Faye said. "But if you're afraid I might tell someone, anyone, ask Bobby."

Johnny gave Faye a hard stare, then looked at me. "Johnny, Faye knew about my underground room for a long time before anyone else. She watched me dig the hole. She saw everything from her upstairs window," I said, pointing next door to Faye's second-story bedroom window.

Faye and her family moved all the way from North Carolina. Though she was a newcomer to the Choctaw Nation, Faye could be trusted. I was certain of that.

"You think your underground room is big enough for my family?" Johnny asked.

"We might have to dig a little deeper," I said.

"And you two are worried about me?" asked Faye.

We all laughed, slapping shoulders and joining in a cool circle of friendship. When the laughter settled, I knew where we should go.

"Time for some deep thinking," I said.

"Kinda hot and dry down there, Bobby. It's summertime," said Johnny.

"I've got that solved," I said. "The ice chest is full of root beer, even some ice cream bars if you want one."

"And don't forget the fan, to stir things up," added Faye.

"Let's go for it," Johnny said.

I dashed to the door, covered with dried leaves, and pulled it aside. My underground room was a secret to all but my closest friends. And my basketball coach, Coach Robison. And Dad and Mom. So, it wasn't as much of a secret as it was a year ago, but it was still a cool place to hibernate and make plans for survival.

As anyone in high school knows, survival is never easy.

I jumped in first and helped Faye wiggle down the sloping side, and then Johnny leapt to the floor. We pulled the door over us, and I flipped the switch on my new battery-operated lantern.

"Hoke," Johnny said. "Now we're safe. No more worries!"

Of course, he was being sarcastic, and I decided to join in.

"Yessiree, Johnny!" I said. "Now, all we have to do is dig another few rooms. A bedroom for your parents and an office for your dad's attorney work."

"And, of course, a television room," said Faye. "And Johnny's mom wants a real kitchen, not just a microwave."

"And maybe we can hire a detective to figure out who unscrewed the top rung of Dad's ladder and sent him to the hospital," said Johnny.

"Oh," said Faye. "Back to reality?"

"That's why we're down here," I said.

We all took a long, deep breath. I popped open the lid to the ice chest, and we each took a cold can of root beer. Two swigs later, I patted Johnny on the knee.

"Any idea who might have done it?" I asked.

"I'm sure Dad has wrestled with dozens of names, men he has convicted and sent to prison. But he would never share that list of suspects with me," Johnny said.

"Faye?" I asked.

"I'm agreeing with Johnny's dad," Faye said. "A convicted criminal looking for revenge will never be satisfied with a hip injury. This is just the beginning."

"Have you really thought about the basketball season, Johnny?" I asked. "You can't just give it up. Basketball is your life—or at least a big part of it."

Johnny gave me a long look, then turned his eyes to Faye. "Since we're beneath the real world, I feel I can open up. And what I'm about to say stays buried. Deal?"

We leaned forward and wrapped our arms around our shoulders, a good old-fashioned circle hug. "Deal," we all whispered.

"All right," Johnny said. "I heard Dad tell Mom that he didn't feel it was safe in our house anymore—for any of us. He said we might need to move."

"Did he say where you might move to?" I asked.

"No, he was just sharing his thoughts with Mom. That's as far as it went."

"And his main thought was not where your family should go," Faye said, "but that *he no longer felt safe.*"

"That's right," Johnny said, "and that's when Mom started crying."

"That would make anybody cry," I said, "to be in danger at your own home."

Johnny looked at Faye. Faye looked at Johnny. Then they both turned their heads and stared at me, waiting for me to realize what I had just said. I lifted my can of root beer and gulped it all down before replying. "Hoke, I get it," I said. "I was in so much danger in my own house, in my own room, and I built a new house. This one."

"Not exactly," Faye said. "You *dug* a new house, Bobby."

After a cool pause for thoughts of the past year, we all shook our heads and belted out a good, long belly laugh. When the laughter floated away, I put my hand on Johnny's shoulder.

"See," I said, "it came out all right."

"Yeah, when your dad stopped drinking. But he had control over what he did. And besides, he would never deliberately hurt you or your mom. This is different. All my family can do is hope and pray that somebody won't burn our house down while we're sound asleep."

Silence. How do you reply to that?

"So, Coach Robison is talking to your dad now?" I asked.

"Yes, and I know Dad has already come up with some plan to keep us safe."

"So, he's either letting Coach know that you can't play this summer, or he's telling him the plan."

"That's what I'm thinking," Johnny said.

We didn't have long to wait. We heard a car pull into the driveway. We pushed the door aside and climbed quickly up to the yard. We knew we would soon hear the news, good or bad. We hurried to the patio and sat around the table.

In less than two minutes, Mom slid open the glass patio door. "Someone would like to talk to you," she said. She stepped aside, and there stood Coach Robison.

"Time for me to practice my dribbling," Faye said. She stood up, waved goodbye to Coach, and left through the back gate.

"Hello, men," said Coach. "Johnny, your dad asked me to tell you that he is feeling much better."

"Thank you, Coach. I appreciate your being there when he needs you."

"He wants to see you this evening," Coach said, "and he will be staying in the hospital for a few more days."

"I thought he was coming home," Johnny said.

Coach took a deep breath and glanced to the door, where Mom was carrying his coffee cup. "One cream and one sugar," she said. She smiled and placed the cup on the table and then stepped back through the door to leave us alone.

Coach kept us waiting as he blew across his cup and took a sip. "Did you ever think growing up would be this hard?" he asked, looking from Johnny to me and back again.

"We grew up a long time ago," Johnny said.

"Yes, you did," Coach replied. "A long time ago."

CHAPTER 4

Safety of the Court

Half a cup of coffee later, Coach Robison continued. "So, let's see what we can do to face this new mountain. Johnny, your dad said he knew you were listening to his conversation with your mother. Do you know the one I'm talking about?"

Johnny's jaw dropped, and he shook his head back and forth. "No way!" he said. "How did…?"

"Son, your dad is a brilliant lawyer. He catches every tiny detail, like the light coming under the door."

Johnny leaned back and laughed, a much-needed laugh, and we joined him. "I love my old man," he said, and I saw tears rising in his eyes.

Coach Robison held up his hand for us to listen. "Your dad is very concerned about your family's safety and is convinced the ladder was deliberately broken. A police guard is watching his hospital room twenty-four hours a day. But the problem, as you know, is what happens when he is released."

"We need to move, don't we, Coach?" Johnny asked.

"Yes, I am afraid so, until the man responsible for your dad's injury is caught."

"But how can we stay hidden?" Johnny asked. "If Dad continues to practice law, anyone can find out where we live. They could follow him home or follow me home from school or basketball practice. Maybe the whole team is in danger."

I saw Johnny's eyes widen as a new and bloodier road ran through his mind.

"Don't get carried away, Johnny," said Coach, patting him on the shoulder. "We do have an answer to the dangers." Coach took another deep breath and another sip of coffee. I reached for Johnny's hand.

"Part of being a great lawyer is knowing how to negotiate, and your dad is one of the best. Once the criminal is caught, he can offer a lesser sentence—but only if no more crimes are committed against your family."

Johnny and I looked at each other with a question in our eyes. Finally, Johnny asked, "Negotiate with who?"

"That's our challenge," said Coach. "The criminal must be caught. And we are not limiting our thinking to someone your dad sent to prison."

"Coach, please let me say this. My dad did not send anyone to prison. What *they* do sends people to prison. The laws send people to prison, not my dad."

"I know, Johnny. Please forgive me," Coach said. "What I mean is that we may not be looking for a criminal. The convicted person may still be in prison, serving out their term. An angry family member might be after your dad."

"That sure broadens the search," I said.

"Yes, it does," Coach said. "So, the police are following clues first and profiles later. And something else you might find interesting, but you have to keep this a secret."

Johnny and I looked at each other, then raised our right hands and nodded.

"Good enough," said Coach. "Hoke, your dad is pretty upset at himself, Johnny. He made sure you had a good camera to catch any movement in the front yard. Anybody that enters your front yard has everything they do filmed, close up."

"Yeah, I remember when he had that camera installed," Johnny said. "It made me pretty nervous since I knew I had to behave."

We both looked at Johnny with wide eyes. Johnny Mackey is the most well-behaved teenager in America. He lowered his head and sighed.

"But no camera in the backyard, is that the problem, Coach?" I asked.

"Yes, so whoever damaged the ladder got away with it."

"For now," Johnny and I said in unison.

"For now," added Coach. "And Johnny, your dad wants you to keep playing basketball. He wanted me to tell you that."

"I will," Johnny said.

"Coach," I said, "it sounds like you want us to be a team, to stay a team. In the investigation, I mean."

Coach lowered his voice before he spoke. He gripped his coffee cup with both hands. "Yes,

Bobby. I hope we can help, and I trust you two young men. And you must consider this, Bobby. If anyone, and I mean *anyone*, discovers you are in any way involved, you put your own family in danger."

"I understand, Coach," I said.

"No sneaking around, no following anyone suspicious."

"What can we do?" Johnny asked.

"Keep your eyes open," said Coach. "This is a small town. Everybody knows everybody. Call me first if you notice anything unusual. Anything."

"Yes, sir," we both said.

Coach left us with a phrase Johnny and I have heard hundreds of times.

"Play clean, play fair, and nobody gets hurt," he said. Then, as we always did before stepping onto the court to begin a game, we all joined hands and cheered.

"Go, Panthers!"

"I'm ready to play some basketball," I said.

"So am I," said Johnny.

"Tomorrow afternoon, after lunch," said Coach. "Two p.m. sharp. For now, our own high school players, the Panthers, and a few Achukmas, from the summer league team. I've already contacted everyone. I'll see you at the gym." Coach took his final swig of coffee and shook our hands as he stepped inside.

"Wow," I said, once Coach was gone. "So, we're now a team of detectives."

"I like it, as long as we stay out of trouble," Johnny said. "Gives me a sense of purpose, something to do to help my dad."

"You know who might be able to help us?" I asked. "Lloyd Blanton. His dad is a recovering alcoholic, like mine, and Lloyd is smart."

"And very observant," Johnny added.

"Yes, he's had to be to survive. When you never know who's about to be shoved or slugged, you have to know everything that's happening around you."

"That's Lloyd."

"Want to go see him now?" I asked.

"Let's wait till tomorrow," Johnny said. "I'm sure he'll be there at basketball practice, and we've got some planning to do."

I stood up and dribbled a few times. "Ready?"

"You bet," Johnny said. "Basketball always makes things better."

In less than ten minutes, we were warming up on the outdoor court, where Dad and I had been. We took free-throws and jump shots, and Johnny even tossed an easy dunk shot through the chain nets. Nothing like the court to bring a player back to life.

"Ready for some one-on-one?" Johnny asked, tossing me the ball. I settled in at the three-point line, rocking back on my left foot.

"You're so much taller than I am, Johnny. I don't know."

Johnny just smiled and eased into his defensive crouch. He knew what I would do— fake to the right and drive hard to my left, throwing up a left-handed hook shot. Since we were on three teams together, the Panthers, the Achukmas, and now the Detective Squad, I decided to make it easy for Johnny.

I gave him exactly what he expected, a hard drive to the left. To no surprise, Johnny waited till the ball left my hand. He soared high over the rim and slapped the basketball with his palm so hard it rolled under a courtside picnic table.

"I'm thinking it's my ball out of bounds," I said, refusing to acknowledge his expert timing on that incredible blocked shot.

"As long as you go fetch the ball," Johnny said.

"No prob," I said. I hurried to the table, dove under it to retrieve the ball, and tossed it to Johnny, as is the habit in one-on-one. He rolled it back to me, and I stayed off court in the corner. Johnny was also ready for my favorite shot in the world, a net-splashing three-pointer.

I took one dribble inbounds, then faded back and reached for the ball, ready to launch the jumper. Johnny took two steps and prepared to slap my second shot away.

Didn't happen. Instead of picking up the ball, I raised both hands high—without the ball. I jumped, Johnny jumped, but I landed first. I took three quick dribbles, driving under the basket for an easy layup.

"Nice try, Johnny."

Johnny shook his head. "I think you have your dad to thank for that one," he said.

"Dad?"

"Yeah. If he hadn't scared the blazes out of you till you ran away from home, you'd never be so good at basketball."

I rolled the ball to Johnny and said in a quiet voice, "Guess you're right. So, now basketball is once again our getaway."

After almost an hour of sweaty outdoor basketball, with both of us winning a few games apiece, Johnny said, "Guess I better be going."

We said very little on the walk home, and when we arrived, Coach was waiting to take Johnny to his house. "Your mom is waiting for you," he told Johnny. "She wants to take you to the hospital to see your dad later today. I know he misses you."

"And what's the news on Dad?" Johnny asked.

"As you know, Johnny, a hip injury is serious," Coach said. "But he's improving, and fortunately no hip replacement will be necessary. Your dad will need you. He's looking at several months of therapy, and no one knows the value of physical therapy like a basketball player."

"Oh, yes, practice makes perfect," Johnny said with a smile. "Maybe you can be his therapist,

Coach Robison—so he'll know what me and Bobby have had to put up with."

"Wow," I said. "Coach, he didn't mean it! I promise."

And the usual Choctaw belly laughs followed. Welcome laughter indeed. I followed Johnny to Coach's car and tapped my heart a few times with my fist as they drove away to let Johnny know I cared for him.

The mountain that Johnny and his family faced was already steep and dangerous, but no one expected a firebomb.

CHAPTER 5

Face the New Mountain

Thirty minutes after they left, Coach's car screeched to a halt in our driveway. *What's going on?* I thought. Coach Robison and Johnny leapt out and hurried up the driveway to our house. Dad heard Coach's car and met them at the door, flinging it open and slamming it quickly behind them.

"What can I do to help?" Dad asked. "What's happening?"

Johnny looked confused and very upset. "Come in and sit down," Dad said.

"The Mackeys are in immediate danger," Coach said as he and Johnny took a seat on the sofa. "Mrs. Mackey is in a patrol car on her way to the police station. We stopped here to let you know of the seriousness of the situation. Bobby, we must be very careful. I think we should assume that no one is safe until the criminals are caught."

Mom and Dad sat side by side. Dad grabbed my arm and sat me between them.

"Johnny," Coach said, "you can tell them what happened better than I can."

Johnny rocked back and forth, with his head bowed and his eyes closed. Coach reached for his hand. "You are among friends, Johnny, people who love you."

"I know," Johnny said. "Yes. Thank you, Coach." He lifted his head and took a deep breath before looking each of us in the eyes. "When Coach brought me home, I told him I'd be hoke. He didn't need to come in. I am so glad that he did. Mom was there, and we both started asking her about Dad. She couldn't answer us fast enough. We were all sitting in the living room.

"After a few minutes, she said she needed a break. She went to the kitchen to bring us something to drink. That's when it happened. We heard the glass shatter. Somebody threw a firebomb, the size of your fist. From over the fence, we think. It busted the kitchen window facing the patio. Glass was everywhere. The bomb rolled like a baseball across the kitchen floor.

"Mom screamed and backed away, but not fast enough. I saw the bomb and threw it out the window, just as it was exploding. The kitchen caught on fire. Coach shoved and carried us out of the house. He called the fire department, and we jumped in his car and locked the doors." Johnny covered his face with his hands and started sobbing.

"I drove down the block," Coach said, "and waited. The firemen were quick to respond, and soon the police arrived. The damage to the house appeared to be minimal. But the Mackeys are no longer safe."

Coach looked to Johnny, almost asking permission to say it. Johnny shrugged his shoulders and hung his head. "The Mackeys cannot live in their own home, not until the criminals are caught."

I lifted my hand to speak.

"Yes, Bobby?" Coach asked.

"What happens now?"

"The police have located a hideaway home in the Kiamichi Mountains, far enough away for now," Coach said. "Mr. and Mrs. Mackey have serious life decisions to make, but for now, day-to-day safety is the major concern."

"Johnny, you know you are always welcome here," Dad said, "but I know you want to be with your family."

"And this is too close to Johnny's home," Coach said.

I tried to imagine the horror of Johnny stepping into his house—after criminals injured his dad—and hearing shattering glass and the explosion of a firebomb in his kitchen. While his mother was there!

"Johnny," I said quietly. He closed his eyes and I walked to his side. I have learned so much from Coach Robison about *seeing the good, even in the darkest hour*. "When you think of today, Johnny, of the firebomb and the explosion, please remember one thing."

Johnny lifted his eyes to mine. We both were crying and letting the tears flow. This was no time to hide from the truth.

"What . . . what," Johnny stammered, "what do you want me to remember?" He was sobbing now, and we joined him.

"You saved your mother's life, Johnny. You threw the firebomb away from her. You showed your love for her and saved her life."

Coach walked over to us and wrapped his strong arms around Johnny and me.

"I am so proud of you young men," he said, burying his head between us and sobbing. But the strength of his feelings came through.

"I know you have very little time," Mom said, "but please stay for just a few minutes longer."

Coach looked up from our tight sobcircle and nodded his *yes*.

"Bobby," Mom said, and I joined her in the kitchen. "There's coffee in the pot for Coach Robison and your dad. Raspberry lemonade for you and Johnny."

I filled the cups with cream for Coach and black for Dad, and filled three glasses with ice-cold lemonade for Mom and Johnny and me. I knew what Mom was doing. She covered five plates with scoops of sweet grape dumplings, made the Choctaw way. Soon Mom and I marched from the kitchen like waitstaff, spreading drinks and platefuls of crumble-crusted Choctaw grape dumplings around our living room.

"A little Choctaw joy never gets in the way," Coach said.

"Even for a Cherokee," Johnny said.

We lifted our glasses high, then bowed our heads as Dad led us in singing "Amazing Grace," in Choctaw and Cherokee both.

"We'd better be going," Coach said, when we finished singing. I gave Johnny a shoulder hug and followed them to the car—but questions filled my mind. *How can Johnny and I work together if I don't know how to reach him? And does this mean he'll not be playing basketball this summer? Or ever again?*

Then I had another thought. Just because I don't know where he is doesn't mean I can't call him. Johnny always keeps his phone with him and it's always charged. Now the problem is *when is it safe to call?*

Totally frustrated, I had to do something. I bolted from the driveway to the living room and tossed the curtains aside. Johnny saw me, as if he knew I'd be there. I did a mime act, putting my hand against my ear like I was talking on the phone, thumb to my ear and little finger to my lip.

Johnny pounded his fist to his chest, letting me know he got the message. Mime act again, I shrugged my shoulders and pointed to my wrist, where folks used to wear their wristwatches.

Johnny responded by pointing first to himself, then to me. *I'll call you first*, he was saying. So now we had our plan, our private plan to stay in touch. Coach Robison at first acted as if he didn't see a thing, but just before he climbed in his car, he turned to Johnny, then to me. He stretched his arms in a big, slow hug, all the time with a serious look on his face.

We both nodded. He was reminding us to keep our promise. *Nobody steps over the line, and nobody gets hurt.*

I stood in the window and waved at Johnny as Coach slowly backed his car out of the driveway. When I turned to go to the living room, Mom and Dad were both standing behind me. "We are as worried as you are," Mom said.

Dad put his arm on her shoulder. "I can't believe this is happening," he said. "Of all the people in town, Mackey is the most professional, the most trustworthy man I know."

"And the most responsible for keeping our town safe," Mom said. "Maybe that's why he is being targeted."

Without saying a word, I hurried out the back door, tossed the door aside, and entered my underground room. I pulled the door over my head and reached for the ice chest. I was glad I had a few cold drinks hiding in the ice. It was hot as blazes!

So, I'll wait till after dark and give Johnny a call, I thought. *He's smart enough to keep his phone on silent so it'll vibrate instead of ring. Then he'll find a quiet place where no one will know we're talking. Hoke. What then?*

Suddenly I had an idea.

I grabbed my phone and called Coach.

"Hello, Bobby. Is everything hoke?" he asked.

"Yes, Coach. I'm in my room and had to give you a call. I know you're driving, but time is important."

"My phone is on speaker, Bobby, so Johnny can hear too."

"Yakoke, Coach. Hoke, we're assuming that since the thugs know where the Mackeys live, they'll be back. Maybe even while Mr. Mackey is still in the hospital."

"Go on," said Coach.

"Hoke, they must know about the camera, and they know that after dark the backyard is the safest entrance."

"I'm with you, Bobby. You're suggesting that the Mackeys have another camera installed, facing the backyard?"

"Yes! And in secret, so the thugs still think they're safe and can't be seen. And it has to be right away. If they're planning more trouble, they'll do it now, before Mr. Mackey is home from the hospital."

"Bobby," Coach said, "you're making a lot of assumptions. But your idea is a good one. I'll swing by the hospital and we'll get going on that."

"Coach, uh, I have another idea."

Johnny jumped in, and it was great to hear his voice. "Sounds like you've got an idea for every dribble, Bobby," he said.

"More like one for every three-pointer," I said.

"Hoke, men," said Coach, "can we get on with it?"

"Right. So, Coach, if they put the backyard camera up right away, it's daylight. Who knows where these thugs might be? Maybe the camera guys can drive a regular pickup truck, maybe dressed as yard workers. So one of them can dig in the flower bed or mow the lawn while the others are installing the camera, somewhere it can't be seen."

I heard Coach laughing and knew that he and Johnny were enjoying the moment.

"Nothing is easy, is it, Bobby?" Coach asked.

"Dad will go for it," said Johnny. "And he'll understand this is gonna cost him a few more bucks. But for our safety, he'll do it. Great idea, Bobby. High five to you!"

"Hoke, I'm driving Johnny to his hideaway home, and I'll make the phone calls within the hour," said Coach.

"Hey, Johnny, have you crossed the Red River yet?" I asked.

"No map-questing, you two," Coach said.

"Naw," said Johnny, "that's still a few hours to the south."

"Oh, hoke. But you've already left the Kiamichi Mountains. I get it."

The long silence gave me the answer I was looking for. They were driving through the mountains. So, Johnny's new home was a mountain hideaway. Makes sense to me.

"We're heading to the Ozarks, Bobby. Now say goodbye."

Since the Ozarks are in Arkansas and they were driving east, Coach was telling the truth. Sort of. "Chipisha Latchiki, Coach. And you too, Johnny."

"See you whenever," Johnny said.

Wait! My underground home is the birthing place of ideas, and I just had another one. I called Coach again. "Coach," I said, "last call. I promise."

"Let me guess," said Coach. "You just remembered that Lloyd's dad has a part-time lawn service business. He only works weekends, but he'll do anything to help the Mackeys."

"That's why you're the coach, Coach."

"Yes, and the player does what the coach says. Bye for now. And good thinking, Bobby." Click.

Now we *are* becoming a team. The Panthers rule! Johnny and Lloyd Blanton—and oh, yeah, his dad too—Coach, and me. Nobody beats us.

Let's hope.

I finished a cold root beer and tried not to worry. I've always been more a *doer* and not a *thinker*, and this was driving me crazy. I threw the door aside and climbed out. As I entered the house, I called out, "Anybody home?"

"We're here," Dad said. "How are you holding up?"

"Doing hoke. I talked to Coach, and he's taking Johnny to his temporary home, as you know. Still don't know where."

"It's better that way, Bobby," Mom said. "And before you sit down, go dry yourself off. You're sweating like a beach boy."

"I don't want to lay around the house," I said. "Mind if I go see Lloyd? We might play some basketball."

"Sure, just be back by suppertime," Dad said. "And no sneaking around!"

"No prob, I'm with you."

As I stepped out the door, Dad called out, "Hey, Bobby, aren't you forgetting something? Your *basketball*?"

"Lloyd's got a basketball," I said. "We'll use his."

"Bobby, have you ever left home without your basketball?" Mom asked.

I had to agree. I backtracked, grabbed the ball, and was soon riding my bike down the sidewalk, switching hands and dribbling as I peddled.

CHAPTER 6

Lawn Worker Spies

Lloyd lived two miles from me, so I soon slowed down to catch my breath. As I neared his house, my mind went back to one of the worst times of my life, certainly one of Lloyd's worst. Earlier this year, Lloyd's mom was in the hospital, recovering from a head-smashing fall on her kitchen floor. Coach Robison picked me up and took me to the hospital, where she had been admitted to the emergency room. She was still unconscious and unable to speak when we arrived.

Our plan was to stay by Lloyd's side and help him survive this nightmare. We quickly made our way to the waiting room, and I will never forget what we saw. Two police officers were questioning Lloyd's dad.

Lloyd looked confused and out of control, and I was afraid he was about to hurt himself, or someone else. "Did your dad come home drunk again?" I asked him.

Coach Robison gave me a stern look, warning me to *take it easy*.

But this was no time to avoid the issue. This was *now or never* time.

Lloyd nodded his head *yes*.

"Did you see what happened?" I asked.

"No, but if the police will just listen to me," Lloyd said, "I know what happened."

"Did your dad do it, Lloyd? Did he shove your mother? Did he hit her?"

"My dad is a drunk. He is a mean and bitter man," Lloyd replied, "and I know what he did to my mother."

"If you were not there, how do you know?" asked Coach.

"I will not say another word until the cops are ready to listen," Lloyd said.

When they finally finished talking to Lloyd's dad, the policemen entered the waiting room.

"Son, we need you to join us," said the older officer, reaching for Lloyd's hand. Lloyd jerked his hand away.

"Anything I have to say, my coach and my friend can hear," Lloyd said. "And I would like my dad to hear me too. I am not afraid of him, and I will tell the truth."

The officers looked at each other, then one turned and walked away. He soon returned, holding Lloyd's dad, Mr. Blanton, by the shoulder.

"Are you ready to answer our questions now?" asked the officer.

Lloyd nodded his head, all the while staring at his dad.

I expected Lloyd's dad to threaten him, to knot up his fist and wave it at his son, to cuss at him. What happened next surprised both Coach and me. Mr. Blanton seemed to relax. He hung his head and waited for Lloyd to speak.

"I knew my dad was drunk when he came home after work. I didn't want to be anywhere near him, so I hurried to my room and slammed the door. I knew Mom was already cooking supper. I heard Dad enter the kitchen and start hollering and cussing, like he always did when he was drunk.

"I heard a loud smashing sound, like Dad was breaking a plate or something. Then I heard my mom cry out. I thought he had hit her, broken her jaw or something worse."

"When you entered the kitchen, where was your mom?" asked the officer. "Was your dad standing over her?"

"Mom was lying on the floor, already passed out," Lloyd said. "But Dad never touched her. He was standing on the other side of the table. Mom slipped and fell. I will swear to it."

Lloyd's dad closed his eyes and shook his head in gratitude and grief. His son, Lloyd, was telling the truth in defense of him.

"You are one lucky man, Mr. Blanton," said the officer.

And indeed he was. As I parked my bicycle and approached the Blantons' door, I recalled why Mr. Blanton finally stopped drinking. He had a near-death experience not long afterward, and at the same hospital.

"Is Lloyd here?" I asked as Mrs. Blanton answered the door.

"Lloyd!" she shouted. "Your friend Bobby is here to see you."

Lloyd knows me. "Tell him to wait in the living room," he shouted back. "I'm putting my basketball shoes on. He does have a basketball, right, Mom?"

Mrs. Blanton smiled and ushered me into the house. "Yes, Lloyd. I've never seen him without it."

Except all those days at the hospital, I thought, but I knew better than to say it.

"We're quite a ways from the court," Lloyd said as we peddled our bikes down the sidewalk. "So, why are you really here?"

"It's about Johnny's dad," I said.

"I thought so. What's up?"

"How is your dad's lawn business going?" I asked.

"What does that have to do with anything?"

"You tell me first, then I'll tell you," I answered.

"Hoke, Bobby Byington. Daddy's doing fine, staying sober and busy. And I'm helping him whenever we don't have basketball practice. Weekends only, just like always."

"You do know that lawyers make a lot more money than your dad or mine, right?"

"Oh, you must mean lawyers like Mr. Mackey, Cherokee Johnny's dad."

"Yes," I said. "And what if your dad can make ten times what he usually does by mowing and cleaning the Mackeys' yard? And you'll be there too, overpaid."

"I'm listening," Lloyd said.

"Hoke, let me first say that *ten times more than usual* is a guess. But here's the plan. The thugs who are after the Mackeys know there's a camera in the front of the house, but none to the rear. And with no camera facing the backyard, they can break into the house and leave a bomb, burn it down, or do whatever kind of evil they want."

"I'm still waiting to know how my dad's lawn business has anything to do with this," Lloyd said.

"Be patient, Lloyd. I'm not launching a three-pointer here, just creating a scenario."

Lloyd pulled his bike to a halt. "Let's hear it," he said.

So I told Lloyd all about the plan to dress the camera installers up like lawn workers. "And they'll be setting up the camera while you and your dad are cleaning up the yard. So even if they're scoping out the house, the thugs will never see what's really going on. Or better yet, if they are watching, I can be close enough to see them."

Lloyd said nothing, just started pedaling again, slowly down the sidewalk.

"What do you think?" I asked, riding behind him.

"Sounds like a win-win to me," he said. "We can use the money, and the Mackeys need the camera."

"So, it's a done deal!" I shouted.

"Yeah, as long as me and you make all the decisions," Lloyd replied.

"At least Coach will listen to us. We'll let him make the pitch to the police. And Mr. Mackey."

We rode in silence till we reached the court, and to our surprise we weren't alone. A van full of older men pulled into the parking lot. On the side of the van we saw the round logo of the State of Oklahoma. Lloyd and I looked at each other, shrugging our shoulders.

"I wonder what's going on?" I said.

"Let's have a seat at the picnic table and watch," Lloyd said.

So, we did. The driver was wearing a uniform, dark blue pants and shirt. He slid open the door to the van and eight men climbed out. Some were gray-haired older men, and others seemed much younger. "Looks like a good outdoor court," said a man in red shorts and a T-shirt.

All the men wore basketball sneakers and were dressed and ready to play.

When he saw us sitting at the table, the driver hollered, "Let's go to other end of the court." He carried a basketball from the van and rolled it across the court.

"Go for it, Billy!" shouted one fellow, and the man in the red shorts ducked his head and broke into a trot. When he reached the ball, he didn't scoop it up, break into a dribble, and drive in for a layup. No, he stopped it with his foot, almost stumbling and falling as he did. He leaned over and took a deep breath.

With his hands on his knees, he looked at his friends and said, "I'm getting too old for this." He knelt down and picked up the ball. "That's more exercise than I've had in a month."

The other men laughed, and the driver said, "That's why we're here, Billy. Time for you guys to get outta the house and exercise."

Lloyd and I walked to the other end of the court and pretended to ignore them. We dribbled and shot short jumpers, moving farther away from the basket with every shot. But I was not ignoring these ballplayers, who came as a group, all arriving in the same van. They were here to exercise, as the driver said—not for the game.

Why are they really here? I asked myself.

Finally, we were arching shots from beyond the three-point line. Several misses and a few swishes later, Lloyd said, "How about a few free throws?"

"Sure thing," I said, tossing him the ball and settling under the basket to rebound.

"Best out of ten?" he asked.

"If you're up for it."

While Lloyd took careful aim and made his first five, I nodded my support, always keeping an eye on the men. Lloyd made eight out of ten, and it was now my turn. As I walked to the free-throw line, I was now close enough to hear what they were saying.

"Let's see you dunk the ball, Billy," one man shouted, tossing him the ball.

"Dunk it?" Billy shouted back. "You know I can't jump that high!"

"Maybe we'll get you a ladder," another man said, laughing and looking around the group.

"Yeah," said another. "I hear you're pretty good with ladders!"

Now everybody laughed and tossed cracks and insults back and forth. Suddenly I noticed something—not everybody was laughing. A young man, the youngest of the group, grabbed the ball and walked slowly to Billy, with a serious look on his face.

"What's this about you and a ladder?" he asked, pushing the basketball against Billy's chest.

"Hey, Tony," Billy said. "You're a friend, a good friend, and you're finally out and back home. Maybe we'll talk about this later."

Everyone froze and watched the confrontation. I dribbled closer to midcourt, still facing Lloyd, so I could better hear everything they said.

"That's enough," shouted the driver. "Don't make me write up a report."

"You do that and you better stay off your roof!" another man hollered.

All eyes went to the man who uttered that last remark. "Over the top?" he asked in a whisper. "Sorry."

I was shocked to hear the ladder and roof comments. I drove to the basket for a quick layup and said to Lloyd, "Let's sit down for a while."

"What's up?' he asked.

"I'll tell you in a minute. This is serious."

CHAPTER 7

Ladders and Criminals

"You sit over there," I said to Lloyd, "so you can see the men from here. But don't let them see you watching them. Hoke?"

"Sure, but what's going on?"

"I knew there was something different about those guys, all arriving in the same van with a uniformed driver. And the driver acts like their boss. So, I kept my eyes on 'em and backed up to midcourt, so I could hear what they were saying."

"What did you hear?"

"They were making jokes about Billy," I said, "the one in the red shorts. One man said he needed a ladder to dunk the ball. Then somebody shouted, 'I hear you're good with ladders,' and *almost* everybody laughed. A younger man, Tony, got very upset with the joking, and he didn't seem to know about the ladder. I just know Billy had something to do with Mr. Mackey's injury. He might be the man we're looking for."

"Who do you think these guys are?" Lloyd asked.

"Maybe they're ex-cons," I said. "Maybe they've served their sentences and are all out on parole. I don't know. The driver might be some sort of officer. I just know the tall one, Billy, had something to do with Johnny's dad."

"How can we find out?"

"I've got a crazy idea," I said.

"That comes as no surprise."

"And you've gotta play too."

"Play what?" Lloyd asked.

"Play basketball! What do you think?"

"Wait," Lloyd asked, "are you telling me we're about to march to the other end of the court and challenge those guys?"

"Not exactly, but here goes."

I tossed the ball to the court and slapped Lloyd on the shoulder. He followed me as I dribbled the ball to the far end, where the men were still shooting.

The driver gave me a curious look, so I walked over to him.

"Me and my friend are high school basketball players. We always come down to this court to play some four-on-four, but nobody else showed up today."

"And you want my men to join you, is that what I'm hearing?" the driver asked.

I shrugged my shoulders. "If it's hoke. Just a game of *first team to ten buckets wins, make it–take it*. Think any of your men will be interested?"

"Let's do it!" shouted a short, muscled-up man. "I can't jump, but I can sure play defense."

"You must have played basketball in high school," I said with a friendly smile.

"Oh, yes."

"And that was how long ago, half a century?" Billy asked.

Everyone laughed at that, and Lloyd jumped in.

"My granddad can still outshoot me," he said. I knew Lloyd was lying. His grandfather had died years ago, but he was showing respect, getting the men to trust him.

Smart thinking, I thought.

The driver lifted his arms to the sky, and what he said next blew me away. He quoted Coach Robison!

"Play hard, play clean, and nobody gets hurt," he said. "So, who wants to play?"

"I'm Bobby and this is Lloyd. My friend and I will split up," I said, "so we need three more players on each team."

"And the two who sit out can sub, if they want to," said the driver. "By the way, my name is Henry Wilson. Just call me Willie. That's what my men call me."

"Nice to meet you, Willie," I said, nodding with respect.

"Me too," said Lloyd.

Mister Red Shorts, Billy, pointed to two men, saying, "We've got our team, and we'll go with Bobby."

"We'll take you on and be on Lloyd's team," said the stout man, pointing to Tony and his other teammate. "And my name is Pete."

So here we were, ready to *play clean, play hard, and nobody gets hurt.*

"You take it out," I said to Lloyd, tossing him the ball. Just as he was about to toss the ball in play, Willie pulled a whistle from his pocket and blew it loud enough to be heard all over the park. We all stopped and stared at him.

"Just a minute here," he said, standing up and puffing his chest out like a military leader giving orders. "We need to have a brief discussion, men. Boys, go shoot at the other end while we talk. Won't take five minutes."

So, Lloyd and I tossed the ball back and forth, then dribbled and trotted to the other end of the court. "What do you think is going on?" Lloyd asked.

"I'm guessing he is reminding them that they will suffer the consequences if anybody gets hurt, especially us. Remember, these men are ex-cons, so they do have anger issues."

"Bobby, you're not sure of anything you're saying," Lloyd reminded me.

"You're right," I said, "but I think that's a safe assumption. Let's shoot from the corners, so we can watch them."

We launched long shots from opposite corners and saw Willie sit the men down at a picnic table. Of course, we couldn't hear a word he said, but he was waving his finger in their faces and speaking in a serious tone of voice. We could see that.

"I was right," I said. "He's warning them."

Twenty shots and five minutes later, Willie shouted, "Come on, boys! We're ready to play."

Lloyd and I ran to half court, and Billy threw me the ball.

"We'll take it in first," he said.

I gave it to Lloyd, who turned around and made sure every player on his team was guarding their man. "Let's go!" he shouted, handing me the ball back.

I knew what I had to do. I threw a high pass to Billy, who stood at the free-throw line. He caught the ball, held it high over his head, and pivoted to his right. The short, strong-armed man, Pete, was guarding him.

"You're not getting around me," he said, challenging Billy.

"You don't know who you're talking to, Pete," Billy said. He gripped the ball with both hands, popped Pete on top of his head, and took two dribbles to his right. Pete was mad. You could see it in his eyes. He backed away for two steps and was about to charge at Billy and tackle him when Willie blew his whistle.

"Turnover!" he shouted. "Billy, you taunted him, you lose the ball. Lloyd, take it out."

Everybody laughed and slapped high fives. Everybody but Billy.

"Hey!" he shouted. "I didn't say nothing!"

"But you popped him on the head," Willie said, "and another word from you and you sit down. We've got two subs here."

So, this is why they don't play sports in prison, I thought. *Too much anger.*

Lloyd threw the ball to Pete, who faked up. When his man left his feet, he shot a ten-foot shot—not a jump shot but just a falling-away, high-arching shot from the baseline. It rattled around the rim and finally dropped through the net.

"Yes!" shouted Lloyd, and all of his teammates joined him.

"Great shot!"

"You did it! Good going!"

Pete showed real class. He shrugged his shoulders and said, "Just luck, but I'll take it."

Willie blew his whistle again.

"He's got to let them know he's still in charge," I whispered to Lloyd.

"Looks that way," he said.

"We're playing make it—take it," he said loudly. "So, Lloyd, your team still has the ball."

This time Lloyd threw the ball to Tony in the corner. Tony took a quick dribble and watched the ball bounce off his shoe and out of bounds. He threw his hands up in the air, frustrated.

"No worries," said Lloyd. "We've still got the lead."

"Not for long," Billy replied.

I have to gain Billy's trust, I thought. So, I walked by him and asked quietly, "You know how to pick-and-roll?"

"Let's do it," he replied.

I threw a high pass, once again, to Billy. But this time he pivoted and tossed the ball over his shoulder to me. He stood with his back to the free-throw line, stout and strong with his feet spread apart. I faked to the left and Lloyd jumped that way, knowing where I loved to drive. I took two dribbles to my left, then spun around and drove back to the right.

Billy knew what I was doing. He kept his right foot planted and turned to face Lloyd, setting a powerful screen. I dribbled as fast as I could, brushing against Billy, and Lloyd was caught. He slammed hard into Billy, who stood his ground.

"Yikes!" Lloyd shouted as he flopped to the ground.

"Sorry. I didn't mean to hurt you," Billy said, reaching for Lloyd's arm to help him up. Then he realized the play was just beginning. "Oops," he said, shrugging his shoulders and looking at Lloyd as he flew to the basket.

I drove to the baseline, and Tony ran hard after me. I flipped a high pass over Tony's arm, and Billy caught it and laid it in.

"I'm saying nothing, not a thing," Billy said, looking at Willie. "No taunting, not from me."

Willie just smiled and shook his head.

"Nice play, son," Billy said as I passed him on the way to the three-point line.

I am not your son, I wanted to say. But Lloyd and I were here for a reason, to protect Johnny and his family. And gaining Billy's trust was key, so I kept my mouth shut. *And what does Tony have to do with this?* I asked myself.

CHAPTER 8

Cons on the Court

The game sped along, with both teams scoring easily. Billy was not the only basketball player from his group. He was the tallest, but Lloyd's team had two players who knew how to dribble and pass, and stout little Pete could score from twenty feet away. Even Tony, once he settled down, showed that he knew how to play this game. He had a nice baseline drive and could score with either hand from anywhere near the basket. He once faked a layup from under the basket, and when Billy left his feet, he pivoted back and scored with his left hand.

"Great shot!" Lloyd shouted.

Pete and Lloyd developed a drive and pitch-back game that opened both of them up for easy, unguarded set shots. Lloyd would drive hard to the basket, and when the defenders crowded around the rim to stop him or at least grab the rebound if he missed, he'd toss the ball back to Pete for a wide-open shot. And Pete would soon return the favor. When Pete hit his third shot in a row from behind the free-throw line, Billy shouted, "Somebody needs to guard him!"

Everybody froze. They first looked at Billy, then all eyes turned to Willie.

Willie said nothing for a long moment, letting the tension build. "Maybe you can show us how," he finally said.

Billy tossed the ball ten feet high in the air and let it bounce on top of his head. No more tension. Everybody cut loose with raucous laughter.

"Yeah, Billy, let's see you do any better!" they shouted.

"Go for it, Billy!"

"Yeah, we wanna see that!"

Billy took a deep breath and tossed the ball to Lloyd. "All right, he's my man from now on."

"I'm shivering in my boots," Pete said, then wished he hadn't.

Pete ran to catch the inbounds pass, as he'd been doing. Billy stayed with him every step, and when Lloyd threw Pete the ball, Billy slapped it away. I caught it before it soared out of bounds. In two quick dribbles, I was at the three-point line. Billy stood under the basket and waved for the ball. I tossed it high and he laid it over the rim.

Back and forth we went, with Pete scoring from the outside and Tony driving for layups. Big man Billy matched them with close-up bank shots, and *yes*, I hit a few three-pointers, from the corner of course.

Lloyd and I were playmakers, enjoying the battle between two *not always* friendly rivals. The men from the van were already relaxing and trusting us, so we had to act like we were here to have fun. And since we were playing basketball on my favorite court in the world, my above-ground rescue court, we were having fun. The most amazing thing to me? Nobody kept score!

After forty-five minutes of play, Willie blew his whistle again. "Time to move along!" he shouted. "I've got an ice chest full of drinks, and you men can use the rest."

All eight of his men agreed, and Pete hurried to the van to carry the ice chest to a nearby picnic table.

"I'm all for that!"

"It's about time we had some R&R."

"Yeah, let's have a cold one. Even if it is soda pop!"

"I guess we better be moving on," I said to Willie.

But I didn't move on. I met Pete at the van and helped him carry the ice chest. As we set the chest on the table, Willie said, "You boys have made this a special day for us. We've got a few extras, so stay around and have a soda."

I looked at Lloyd and he shrugged his shoulders.

"Sounds cool," I said.

So, we joined the men at the tables. Lloyd knew I'd want to learn all I could from Willie, the leader and boss, so he sat with Billy and his teammates at the other table. It was close by, but far enough away for some privacy. I hoped.

We popped the caps from our drinks and took long sips. "You boys must live nearby," Willie said.

"Yeah, and we both learned how to play on this court. We still play here a lot."

"I'm guessing you're on the local high school team," he said. "You're too good just to be playgrounders."

"Uh-huh. Lloyd and I are both guards on the Panthers. We're staying in shape, hoping to have another good year," I said.

I wanted so bad to ask my questions, to dig out whatever information I could. But I know that waiting is sometimes best. So, I just looked around at the men sitting at the other table, then looked back at Willie. He read the question in my eyes.

"Yeah, some of these men played high school ball. That was a lifetime ago." He was about to say something, then stopped himself. "Well, we've all been through tough times in our lives. You two are young, but I'm sure you've not had perfect family lives," Willie added, raising his eyebrows.

"Far from perfect," I said, "but my dad quit his drinking, and life seemed to change overnight."

"Drinking, huh?" Willie asked. "So, you've been through that and survived. You know, if I had to guess, most of the men in the prison system came from houses like yours. You are very fortunate, Bobby."

I waited.

"I see these fellows several times a week," Willie went on. "Mostly alone, sometimes in small groups. Everybody needs support."

"Lloyd's dad, mine too, have had run-ins with the law. Is there any way you can steer them to a group like yours?" I asked.

Willie knotted his fist and covered his mouth with it, looking very uncomfortable.

I've gone too far, I realized. *Better change the subject.*

"That's a cool uniform," I said. "You must be on the police force."

He relaxed and smiled. "Glad you think so, Bobby. That's why I bought it, to give me that extra look of authority. No, I'm not on the force. I bought this at a local clothing store. Anybody can buy a blue uniform."

"Wow," I said. "It does look cool, and I sure wouldn't want to cross you. And neither would my dad."

Willie tilted his head and gave me a look that said, *You're not gonna leave that alone, are you?* He then reached for his whistle with his right hand. His left hand slipped into his shirt pocket.

Willie blew the whistle and shouted, "Hey, Billy, did you keep score?"

All eyes went to Billy, and Willie quietly slipped me his business card. I tucked it away in my pocket before anyone saw.

"I was about to keep score," Billy said, "but your whistle interrupted me."

"Yeah, lucky for you," Pete said, ducking as Billy leaned over the table and tossed him a slow and comical fist. More laughter.

"Men, let's head to the house," Willie said. "Boys, we hope to see you again sometime, and good luck with the coming basketball season."

"Go, Panthers!" several men shouted.

Lloyd and I hopped up and waved as we walked to our bicycles.

"Any luck?" Lloyd asked, once we were out of hearing. I jumped on my bike and peddled half a block before I answered.

"We got what we hoped for," I finally said. "Willie and I had a brief talk about tough times growing up, and he gave me his business card."

"Are you serious?"

"Yes, but let's keep it quiet," I said. "I kinda sorta lied."

"What did you tell him?"

"I told him our dads had had trouble with the law and might need some help."

"Not totally untrue," Lloyd said.

"Also, not totally true," I added.

"What happens next?" Lloyd asked.

"Well, let's see what's going on with Johnny and his family. Man, how much can Johnny go through? First his dad falls and almost breaks his hip, then somebody throws a bomb in his house. Now the whole family has to move away and nobody knows for how long."

We soon eased our bikes from sidewalk to driveway, leaned them against the garage, and entered the house. "Welcome home!" Mom shouted from behind the closed door of her office. "Grab anything you like from the fridge. Just keep it quiet for a while."

"So, no TV?" I asked.

"Hoke, Bobby," Mom replied. "I'll pop on my headphones—and no knocking on my door unless the Russians are coming. You understand?"

I understood, but the look on Lloyd's face told me he didn't have a clue.

"It's an old movie—*The Russians Are Coming.* It was a comedy," I explained, "but when Mom was growing up, everybody in America was afraid the Russians were about to bomb us."

"That explains everything," Lloyd said, and we headed to the kitchen.

"It also means there's no news about Mr. Mackey, or we'd have heard it. But it would be nice to know where Johnny is," I said, pulling my phone from my pocket and dialing his number.

I was just about to hang up when Johnny answered. "Can't talk long," he said. "And Coach made me turn off all tracking apps, so don't even try to locate me. And yeah, I'm safe. Mom will soon join me, after she visits Dad at the hospital."

"How do you know she won't be followed?" I asked.

"They've thought of that," Johnny said. "She is taking a roundabout road through the hills, escorted by undercover police in a regular car, so they'll catch anybody trying to follow her."

"Man, I'm really sorry about all this," I said. "And tell Coach to give me a call when he can. Tell him it's important. Not urgent, but important."

"Will do. Goodbye for now," Johnny said as he hung up.

Lloyd and I high-fived and said goodbye to the day's adventure, and he sailed his bike down the driveway.

CHAPTER 9

Welcome Detective Hancock

An hour later Coach Robison called. "Is your dad home, Bobby?" he asked.

"No, Coach. Are you back in town?"

"Yes," Coach said, "and I'm asking you not to call Johnny. Not yet. I'll call your dad and see when we can meet at your house."

"That's great, Coach. I do have some new information."

"Save it for now. I'm hoping to see you in a half hour, and the detective assigned to the case is coming over too."

"The detective?" I asked. "He's coming here?"

"Yes, Bobby," Coach said. "I want your parents to know what's going on, and I want to make sure you don't do something crazy and get yourself hurt. And you need to understand, when you put yourself in danger, the entire Mackey family is also at risk."

"Yes, sir," I said. Coach was right. "I am sorry to make you worry. We are way out of our league here."

"Yes, you are, Bobby. See you soon."

Dad arrived first and Coach soon after. Mom pulled extra chairs around the kitchen table, Dad made coffee, and Coach shared the news on Mr. Mackey.

"He is still unable to walk by himself," he said. "His hip was badly damaged, and he's hobbling around with a walker. I helped him get out of bed and go to the restroom, and he was in a lot of pain."

"Is Mrs. Mackey with him?" Mom asked.

"Yes," said Coach. "For now. They have her set up in a private room next door to the hospital, for visitors of long-term patients."

"Long-term?" Dad asked.

"Yes. He is not long term, but there is privacy, and the facility is guarded." Coach took a long sip of coffee, and as he set his mug on the table, he tilted his head to me. "You did mention you had some information to share, Bobby," he said.

"Oh! I almost forgot," I said, reaching in my pocket for Willie's business card.

Just then the doorbell rang.

We didn't hear his car pull up to the curb, but the detective had arrived. Dad sprung to his feet, and Coach peered through the window.

"Yes, that's him," he said. Then he turned to me. "Bobby, hold off on your information till we hear what the detective says."

"Sure thing, Coach," I said.

Dad opened the door and welcomed our guest. "I'm Duke Byington," Dad said. "And I think you know Coach Robison."

"Yes, we have met," he said, nodding to Coach. "I am Officer Hancock, and thank you for inviting me. I'm a detective on the police force."

"My wife and son, Bobby, are waiting for us in the dining room," Dad said. Soon we all sat in a circle.

"You must be the famous Bobby Byington," Detective Hancock said with a smile.

"Sounds like he's already been warned," Coach said.

"So without wasting time, here's where we are," Detective Hancock said, and everyone grew quiet. "Someone loosened the screws on the top rung of Mr. Mackey's ladder, either early morning or late the night before. We feel certain this was done deliberately to harm Mackey. Our primary suspects are men he has prosecuted and sent to prison. There are eight suspects that live within fifty miles. But we are not limiting our suspects to actual inmates on parole.

"The criminal, or criminals, might be either friends *of* or related *to* the inmate. And our fear is that, since the attack occurred at the Mackey residence, the family is in danger. You may also know that Johnny Mackey has been moved to another location. Coach Robison here knows the location, but is sworn to secrecy. And I must request that if any of you discover where they are, please call me and let me know your source of information.

"And I must have your assurance that none of you, including you, Bobby, will do any investigating or ask any questions, or in any way interfere with my work. Can I have that promise?" he asked, pointing his hand at each of us as he moved around the circle.

We all answered *yes*.

"Now," Detective Hancock continued, "I cannot guarantee an answer, but I am ready to hear your questions."

"You are absolutely certain this was no accident?" Mom asked.

"Without a doubt, this was a deliberate attack," Hancock replied.

"Are you investigating the alibis of the suspects?" Dad asked.

"We are, and a few alibis cannot be confirmed. Also, lies to protect the guilty are not uncommon among prison parolees and friends."

"I am assuming you are here for a reason," Dad said.

"I am," Detective Hancock said. "I am aware of the close personal relationships you all share, with each other and the Mackeys. I am hoping you may know something that can help us."

I looked from Dad to Coach and back again, wondering if now was the time to share what I had learned. My looks did not go unnoticed.

"Do you have anything to say, Bobby?" Hancock asked.

"Yes, Detective Hancock," I said. "First, I have a confession to make. I had a plan, which I promise I will never follow through on. Not now. I told my friend Lloyd that his dad could pretend to be mowing the Mackeys' lawn while a backyard camera was being installed at their house. That way the criminal would never know he was on camera if he returned."

"Bobby, that backyard camera was installed last night, well after dark. The criminals know nothing of it. And let's keep it that way. No mention of it to Lloyd or anyone. Are we clear?"

"Yes, sir, I promise."

"Anything else?"

"Yes, Detective. While Lloyd and I were at the outdoor basketball court, just an hour ago, a van pulled up. A man in a uniform was driving, and he seemed to be the boss. Eight men were in the van, and they were there to play basketball and exercise."

"And why are they of interest?"

"They seemed to be ex-cons," I said. "I don't know why, but that's what they looked like to me. And I heard one say that Billy, the biggest and strongest of the group, was 'really good with a ladder.' They joked back and forth about it."

"Can you connect Billy with the Mackeys' ladder?" Detective Hancock asked.

"I think so," I said. "They didn't know we were listening, since we were shooting baskets at the other end of the court. One of the ex-cons, a young man they called Tony, grew really angry when he heard Billy joking about the ladder. They were about to fight when the boss man, Henry Wilson— the man they call Willie—blew his whistle and made 'em stop. Billy said something about doing it for Tony, his friend. But Tony was furious."

"Go on," Hancock said.

"Me and Lloyd gained their trust, and we scrimmaged with them for a while. Then we sat down and had sodas with the group. Their leader, Willie, gave me his business card."

"Why?" Hancock asked.

"I told him a lie and said my dad had a run-in with the law and might need his help."

"Bobby, you told him that?" Dad asked.

"Dad, he didn't know who I was."

Detective Hancock leaned back and glanced from Dad to me and back again, letting us know this was not the time for a father-son squabble.

"Do you still have this card?" he said.

I nodded and handed it to him.

"So, you think this Billy may be the man who tampered with Mackey's ladder?"

"Yes," I said. "He bullied everybody in the group and had to be warned by Willie. And Tony may be the man Mr. Mackey prosecuted."

"Bobby, I must ask you again," Hancock said. "Can you keep a secret?"

"Yes, Detective. You have my word."

"We will include Willie and his group in our investigation," Hancock said.

"And you'll tell him nothing about this conversation?" Dad asked.

"You have my assurance on that," Hancock said, rising from the table. "So, if you have nothing more to add, I'll be on my way. I will keep you informed as much as I am allowed, without endangering the investigation."

"Thank you, Detective Hancock," Dad said. as he ushered him out the door. He then turned to us and said, "I feel like we have one smart detective on our side."

"I agree," said Coach.

"Coach, Lloyd and I did our jobs well, didn't we?" I asked.

"I'm very proud of you two young Panthers," Coach answered. "You stayed out of the way of danger, you kept quiet, and still added important information."

"Most importantly," Dad added, "you stayed out of danger. Now let Detective Hancock do *his* job."

"Sure thing, Dad." I ambled out the back door as Coach and Dad smiled and shook their heads, knowing where I was headed. There's no place on earth like my underground home.

CHAPTER 10

Where Do We Go from Here?

Watching as always from her upstairs window, Faye soon appeared. Not a surprise. She had seen me enter my underground hideaway. She knelt down and spoke to me through the plastic pipe, our above-ground sound source. "Need some company?" she asked.

"If you've got cheesecake," I replied. I was joking, of course, but Mystery Lady Faye had a way of always coming through. She didn't say a word in reply, but less than ten minutes later she knocked on the door.

"Mind giving me a hand?" she asked.

"You have got to be kidding me!" I said. My eyes opened wide, as she expected.

When I tossed the door aside, there she stood, holding a small paper plate in each hand, with strawberry cheesecake and two plastic forks.

"You ask, and it shall be answered," Faye said.

I took the plates as she climbed inside. "There's nobody like you. Anywhere in the world."

"Thank you, Bobby Byington," she said. "Now, if you'll close the overhead door, we can enjoy our cake."

As we gobbled and washed the cheesecake down with ice-cold root beers, I told Faye everything that happened today. *If Detective Hancock knew her, he'd trust her too,* I thought.

"I guess there is nothing we can do now," she said. "Just keep our eyes open and wait." And wait we did. When the light gave way to darkness, she climbed from my room, but not before giving me a warm goodbye hug.

As I entered the living room, Mom and Dad were watching television. "Anything on the news?" I asked.

"No," Dad said, "and I would be surprised if Detective Hancock allowed any information to reach the press. Any attempts to interview the Mackeys would have everybody asking, *Where did they go?*"

"They sure don't want that," said Mom.

"Guess I'll head to bed," I said. "It's been a long day. I just hope Johnny is safe."

"Coach Robison and his friend, Detective Hancock, will make sure of it, Bobby," Dad said. "Get some rest and try not to worry."

Easier said than done, but I thought I'd give it a try.

Not. Gonna. Happen. An hour after the lights went out, the doorbell rang.

Ding-dong, ding-dong.

I rolled out of bed and tossed on my jeans and a T-shirt. I tiptoed across my room, quietly opened the door, and peered around the corner, looking to see what Dad would do. He stood to the side of the front door and didn't turn any lights on. Finally, he asked in a loud voice, "Who is it?"

"It's Detective Hancock. I need to speak to you, and please keep the lights out. I'm here alone. Can I come in?"

Dad opened the door and Hancock entered quickly, then shut the door behind himself.

"I didn't want to risk a phone call," he said, "knowing you'd probably turn on your light before answering. Go now, please, and tell your wife and son to stay quiet and in the dark."

Dad was in and out of their bedroom quickly, and I stepped into the living room just long enough to say, "I'm cool, Dad."

"Get back to bed, son," Dad said.

I shut the door but stayed close enough to listen.

"What's the emergency?" he asked.

"We think we may have a lead on who is after Mackey," Hancock said. "And your son gave us the clues we were looking for. He was correct to suspect the man from the basketball court. I called Willie, as he calls himself, and got a list of the men he took to the park. It turns out Billy Randell is on parole for armed robbery. His friend Tony was also convicted for robbery, and the prosecuting attorney was Mackey."

"Did Willie ask how you got his name?" Dad asked.

"No, but he's a smart man. He has to keep a keen eye on everything going on around him to survive. That's one reason I dropped by. Be careful. Until we solve the crime and put a halt to this, no one is safe."

"Why do you think Willie gave Bobby his card?"

"Here's what I really think is going on," Detective Hancock said. "Willie cannot make any accusations or report suspicions he may have. He'd be spending his whole life filling out reports. But I think he knows that Billy is involved. He wants to help us."

"Can you leave me a photo of Billy or anyone else you suspect?" Dad asked. "I'd feel much better knowing who to avoid."

"Do you own a gun?" Hancock asked.

"Yes, a hunting rifle," Dad said, "but I haven't used it in a few years."

"I do not want you to use it," Detective Hancock said. "I want you to promise me that you will call law enforcement if and when you see Billy. Do not take justice into your own hands. You have no authority and you can be charged."

"I can guarantee you, this is between you and the criminals. Not me and my family," Dad said.

"Good," said Hancock. "I would not be here if I wasn't sure I could trust you. I also have a message from Mr. Mackey. He asked me to tell you he's lucky to have friends like you."

"Thank you," Dad said.

"I do apologize for this late-night visit. It's time for me to go. I'll see that you get a recent photo of Billy tomorrow."

Dad raised his eyebrows and Detective Hancock read his mind.

"Why wait?" he said. "You're right. What's your email address?"

Dad left the room and soon returned with his business card. "I've circled the best email. It's private," he said, handing the card to Hancock.

"I'll phone my office," Hancock said, "and you'll have the photo in ten minutes. You can download and print it." He was about to go, but then he paused and took a breath. "Always seems like there's *one more thing*," he said. "Mr. Byington, I know you will want to give a copy of the photo to Bobby. I will allow that, to keep Billy fresh in his mind. But no one else can know we are on the lookout for Billy.

If he hears we are aware that he may be involved in the crime, he can disappear from sight. We don't want that. Eyes open, mouths silent."

"I agree and understand," Dad said. "Thank you for your work."

Detective Hancock quietly nodded and was soon gone. I peered through my window, trying to catch a look at his car. I wanted to see if he was driving a patrol car or an unmarked vehicle, but I saw nothing. No taillights, no lights on inside his car. No car. Nothing.

Dad opened the door to my room, which he almost never did without knocking. "Bobby," he whispered, "I don't want to wake up your mother. I know you were listening to our conversation, so don't pretend you weren't. I will share the photo of Billy with you tomorrow morning, but you are to show it to no one. Do you understand?"

"What about Coach Robison?" I asked.

Dad was silent for a moment. "I will email Detective Hancock and ask him to send one to Coach. That's not our business."

"Yes, Dad," I said. "It just makes sense."

"Yes. Now, son, it's past your bedtime."

"Night, Dad."

"Night, Bobby."

Hours later we enjoyed a nice breakfast of scrambled eggs and French toast, with my favorite raspberry syrup. I tossed down what was left of my cranberry juice and set my glass down in front of Dad.

"Be patient, Bobby," he said. "I haven't opened my email yet."

Mom just looked from me to Dad and back again, so I knew he'd already talked to her about the photo. And, of course, my mind was sailing like a house in a hurricane, spinning and dipping and looking for a place to land. Finally, I found the best landing spot—my underground home!

Mystery Lady Faye has to see the photo of Billy, and so does Lloyd, I thought. *That's where we'll meet after Dad prints out the picture.*

CHAPTER 11

Billy Makes the Rounds

Soon after breakfast Dad handed me an 8½-by 11-inch envelope. "Don't leave the house with this, Bobby," he said. I nodded *yes* and hurried to my room—my other room. I sat at my desk and pulled out the photo. It was Billy, no doubt about it.

I had expected the kinds of pictures you see criminals pose for after they're arrested: two black-and-white photos, one from the side and one facing the camera. Instead, this picture was in full color, and though he wasn't smiling, Billy looked friendly, with bright blue eyes and brownish-blond hair.

"You're not fooling me," I said aloud.

I heard Dad start his truck, and as he backed down the driveway, I hustled through the kitchen, glad to see Mom was still in her office. Leaning the envelope against the tree trunk, I pulled the door aside, grabbed the picture, and entered my underground home. With the door roof closed, I flipped on my flashlight and waited.

"Five minutes, maybe less," I said.

"Way less, Bobby," Faye said, speaking through the pipe. "Mind if I join you?"

"Your wish is my command," I replied, lifting the door aside. Faye leapt in and helped me replace the roof.

"Something for me?" she asked, tilting her head and glancing at the envelope. I pulled out the photo.

"Ever seen this man?" I asked.

"Are you kidding me, Bobby?"

"No, I'm asking a serious question. Have you ever seen this man?"

"Of course, I have seen him. He volunteers several times a month. He and his friends, mostly older men, pick up trash on the road leading out of town."

"Oh, so he lives around here?" I asked. I decided to play detective rather than share what I knew, at least for now.

"I don't know where he lives, but I have seen him driving around town. Recently, now that I think about it."

"Oh, yeah. He drives that bright-red convertible."

"Bobby! Either you're blind or making this up. First, you tell me why you have his picture, then I'll tell you what he drives."

"You first," I said, taking back the picture.

"Bobby, you're acting more weird than usual. But all right, he drives an old white Chevy pickup truck."

"Faye, you have to promise me that you will tell no one about this picture."

"Top secret," she said.

"Hoke. His name is Billy, and he is out on parole. One of his cellmates was a man Johnny's father convicted and sent to prison. He is a suspect in Mr. Mackey's injury. When did you see him last?"

"Bobby, I saw him driving through the neighborhood a few days ago."

"Before the ladder broke?" I asked.

"I can't swear to it. Oh, Bobby, we are no longer safe. If he and his friends find out we are working with the police, they can come after us."

"So, you see why secrecy is more important than ever?"

"Yes, I do. What can we do?" she asked.

"Well, whenever we have information, we need to share it. Normally I would call Coach, but we had a visitor late last night. A Detective Hancock knocked on our door and sent this picture to Dad by email. He gave Dad his card and asked him to call if we heard anything about this man Billy."

Faye had a look on her face I rarely saw. She looked afraid.

"I'll call Dad," I said. The phone rang only once.

"Is everything all right, Bobby?" Dad asked.

"Yes, but we've got some news. Faye is with me."

"You showed her the picture, didn't you, Bobby?"

"Dad, it's a good thing I did. She has seen this man around town several times. He drives a white Chevy pickup, and she saw him driving by a few days ago. Detective Hancock needs to know."

"Tell her thank you, Bobby. I will call Detective Hancock right away. And neither of you go anywhere till you hear from me."

"I understand, Dad." I hung up the phone and looked at Faye. She had her hands folded over her face.

"Faye, don't let your imagination get carried away. No one is after us, and Johnny is safe. Dad is calling the detective. He said for us to wait till he gets here."

She unfolded her hands and gave me a very nervous smile.

Twenty minutes went by, or should I say crawled by? Dad knocked on the door and pulled the door aside. "Come join us on the porch," he said.

Detective Hancock was standing on the porch. "Best if we step inside," he said.

Soon we gathered around the kitchen table. Hancock placed the picture of Billy in front of Faye. "Are you certain this is the man you saw?" he asked.

"Yes," Faye replied.

"How many times and where exactly?" he asked.

"I saw him first maybe a month ago. He was with a group of men, eight men. They were picking up trash by the side of the highway going out of town."

Detective Hancock raised his eyebrows. Dad and I looked at each other, reading his mind. I nodded at Dad and he spoke. "Faye has a memory you can count on," he said. "If she says *eight*, that's how many men there were."

Detective Hancock nodded and smiled. For the first time, he actually smiled!

"And you saw him driving through the neighborhood? What time of day?" he asked.

"Yes, I saw him driving an old white Chevy pickup, maybe ten years old. It was just before dark as I was walking home from the library."

"Which direction was he driving?"

"He was going east on Cooper Street, Johnny's street. I stood on the corner and watched him pass before I crossed the street."

"Was he alone?"

"Yes, and he was talking on his phone, driving real slow and checking house numbers."

"How do you know that?" Hancock asked.

"If the house number was easy to see, he drove right by. If the number was small and hard to see, he pulled to the curb and searched till he found it. I remember wondering why he didn't just call whoever he was meeting."

"Faye," I said, "you never told me this."

"Now you know why I have been afraid, Bobby. This man Billy has been patrolling the neighborhood."

Detective Hancock cleared his throat and looked at Dad.

"Bobby, we are here to listen," Dad said, and I shrunk in my seat and zipped my mouth shut.

"Thank you, Mr. Byington," Hancock said. "And young lady, we are keeping an eye on the suspect 24/7. More than ever, you must keep our conversations a secret. I cannot tell you our plans, but they depend on your secrecy."

"Yes, I understand," Faye said.

"And Bobby?"

"Yes, sir."

"Mr. Byington, may we step into your office?" Hancock asked.

"Certainly," Dad said, leading him to the office and closing the door behind him.

"What are they talking about?" Faye whispered.

I leaned close to her before speaking. "If you look outside, there's no car in the driveway. You couldn't see that from where you were sitting.

Detective Hancock is making sure Billy doesn't know he is talking to us. If he or any of his friends drove by and saw a police car, we might become targets."

"My next question should be obvious," Faye said, and I had to smile.

"Uh, let me guess," I said. "You're wondering how he got here and how he's going to get away. Did I guess right?"

"You win the grand prize, Bobby! A knock on the head."

"I guess I earned that," I said, relieved to see the fear floating away. For now. "Detective Hancock is calling for the patrol car that dropped him off. I'm guessing in less than two minutes he will hurry to the curb, jump in the car, and neither honk nor wave as he drives away."

I was right. As we moved to the living room, Detective Hancock left Dad's office and ran in front of us like a husky fullback dashing for a touchdown. Out the front door he went, into a dark unmarked police car parked by the curb. Just as I predicted.

CHAPTER 12

Achukmas Again!

Coach Robison called early that afternoon, and Dad handed me the phone. "You're not forgetting we have basketball practice today, Bobby?" Coach asked.

"I wasn't sure, Coach, after everything else that's happening," I said. "But I'm ready to play. Will everybody be there?"

Coach Robison had selected the players for our team—the Achukmas, an all-Indian team for a summertime national high school tournament. Our team included some of the best high school basketball players from across the state of Oklahoma, All-State players from several tribal nations. Johnny Mackey and I were the only local players on the team, he being Cherokee and me Choctaw. Our high school team, the Panthers, often practiced with the Achukmas.

"Mato, Eddie, and Jimmy will be there," Coach said. "And Lloyd and several other Panthers will join us, so we can play five-on-five full court."

"Two o'clock at the gym?"

"Yes," Coach said, "and I expect you to be dressed, ready to play, and on the court by two o'clock, Bobby."

"Be great to get going again," I said, and I meant every word.

"And something else, Bobby," Coach said. "When you arrive at the school parking lot, you will see Johnny's car, the dark-green Subaru."

"Johnny will be there?" I asked, excited to see my best friend again!

"No, Bobby," Coach said, "Johnny is still in hiding. But I left my car at his new home—his temporary home—and I will be driving his car. And Bobby, this was Detective Hancock's idea. The criminals know Johnny's car, and if they're looking for where he and his mother are staying, they might spot it."

"But won't they see his car at school?" I asked. "If Billy and his thug friends are looking for Johnny, they'll think he's here."

"That's what we are hoping, Bobby. An unmarked police car will also be in the parking lot. The officers will be looking for a white pickup truck, the one belonging to Billy. So, it is very important that neither you nor Lloyd say a word about Johnny's car. Keep quiet about this. Understand?"

"Yes, Coach, and it sounds like a smart plan to me."

"Well, I would never have approved of it," Coach said. "Bringing the criminals to our school is bringing the danger close to home. But if it helps catch the thugs who are after Johnny's family…"

"Does Dad already know?" I asked.

"Yes, your dad and mother both know," Coach replied, "and they're keeping quiet about it."

After we said goodbye and I hung up, I thought about what could happen. I agreed with Coach. Why bring the danger close to home? We had no idea what Billy and his thug friends might do.

As Dad dropped me off, I saw Johnny's car but pretended not to notice it. I also spotted the blue van and waved to the driver. He carried players from other cities to our scheduled practices. The out-of-towners like Lakota Mato and Creek Eddie usually stayed overnight. That's how we became a real team. We got to know each other on and off the court and could practice for several hours, afternoon and early morning.

I entered the gym and stepped to the court, and my basketball friends waved and greeted me. "Hey, Bobby, how ya been?" shouted Mato as Creek Eddie scooped up a basketball and threw it the length of the court. It rolled to my feet.

"Let's see if you can still shoot the long shot!" he said.

"No problem," I said, and I dashed to his end of the court, dribbling between my legs and around my back as I ran. Three dribbles past midcourt, I tossed up a thirty-foot running jump shot. It missed everything, but Mato, our post player, caught the ball and laid it in. Soon all ten players were shooting, passing, defending, shot-blocking, and enjoying our basketball world.

At five minutes till two, Coach Robison blew his whistle.

WHRRRRRrrrrrrrr.

"Time to get started, men," he shouted. "I am sure you are all aware of the dangers facing Johnny Mackey and his family. We will discuss how that affects us later. For now, let's play basketball. Warm-ups first. Everybody at the baseline, far end of the court. When I blow the whistle, start running to the other end. When I blow it again, run backward till you hear the whistle."

We ran back and forth, backward and forward, for ten minutes. We were breathing hard and glad when Coach blew his whistle and shouted, "Have a seat, men!" We gathered at the bottom of the bleachers.

"Catch your breath for a minute. We'll do layups first, right and left side, ten each, then jump shots starting at the free-throw line and moving out." He walked across the gym, lifted two basketballs from the rolling ball rack, and tossed them on the court.

"Time to hit some shots. Let's go!"

We dashed to the court, excited to dribble and drive and sink our layups. With every shot I thought of Johnny and I missed him. He always rebounded my layups, and sometimes as a joke he blocked my shot before it hit the backboard. Coach saw the look on my face. He casually strode over and stood beneath the goal. As I drove to the basket with my left hand, he jumped behind me and slapped the ball as it left my hand.

"Feel better now, Bobby?" he asked, grinning like he never did at practice.

"Choctaw mind reader," I whispered. "You knew I was thinking of Johnny."

Warm-ups went well, with Eddie tossing in those high-arching three-pointers he was known for. Our Lakota big man, Mato, even made a few. I was happy with my shooting, as five of my ten shots from behind the line settled at the bottom of the net.

Coach blew his whistle and shouted, "Time for some half-court. Eddie, Mato, Bobby, Jimmy, and Lloyd, you're on one team—the Achukmas—for today. Panthers, you take the ball out first. First team to ten baskets, make it–take it. And remember, play hard, play clean, and nobody gets hurt."

We settled into a man-to-man defense, and as my man received the inbounds pass, I guarded him closely, swatting at the ball as he dribbled. He soon threw the ball to a teammate, and I saw something unusual from the corner of my eye. Coach Robison pulled his phone from his pocket. He never carried his phone during practice.

He turned his back to us and walked quickly to his office, the phone to his ear. In less than a minute, he opened his office door and shouted, "Keep playing till I return, men. I won't be long. Call your own fouls and your defense is up to you."

As he shut the door, I smiled. I knew exactly why he added that last phrase about "defense is up to you." If he wanted to take our minds off the troubles, and the possibility of the emergency call, giving *us* the right to decide our defense would do it. Full-court press, tight man-to-man, zone defense, and we get to choose!

"Mato," I shouted, "are you up for a full-court press?"

"I'm all for it," Mato said. "All I've got to do is stand under the basket and block every shot they try."

"Let's do it!" shouted Eddie. He was small and quick and loved the fast game. Lloyd knotted his fist and waved it high.

"Hey, Bobby Byington," shouted James, my Panther teammate. "Are you forgetting you're one of us too?"

"No way I'll ever forget that," I said. "It's all in good fun and makes us better players. You guys can full-court press if you want to."

Nice reminder, I thought. *Remember, Bobby, don't get too big for your britches. And don't leave your friends behind.*

"We'll take it at midcourt," James said. He stepped out of bounds and tossed the ball to Bart, and was I in for a surprise! Bart was a guard, a playmaker. He was an hoke shooter, but his ball-handling skills were not so good. When Lloyd had a bad ankle sprain, just before we played in the district championship game, Bart took Lloyd's place. He couldn't dribble without bouncing the ball off his foot. Our opponents stole the ball from Bart so many times we didn't have a chance, and we lost the district championship.

"Like stealing candy from a baby," my Choctaw granddad used to say.

As soon as Bart caught the ball, Eddie hurried to Bart's left. I left my man open and ran to Bart's right. We waved our arms high, so he couldn't pass over us. And he didn't throw the ball over our heads. No.

Bart, lousy ball-handler Bart, acted confused, with *Which way do I go?* written all over his face. When we reached him, planning to trap him and slap the ball away, Bart never picked up the ball. The confused look left his face, and he bent down low, close to the court. Still dribbling, and not looking at the ball, he flung a hard dribble between us, right between Eddie and me. The ball hit the court hard and bounced ten feet high!

We were running so hard we couldn't stop quick enough. He dashed through us, picked up the ball, and drove in for a layup. Or so he thought! Mato was waiting there to block his shot and send it sailing to the stands. Or so we thought!

Bart was ready. He faked up, Mato left his feet, and Bart tossed the ball to James, who was waiting under the basket.

Yeah! Go, Panthers, GO! they all shouted. I had to laugh, a good-natured Choctaw belly laugh, full of respect.

"Nice play, Bart," I said and shook his hand.

"Yeah, great play," James said. "Thanks for the dime."

Bart just took it all in, nodding and enjoying what was maybe his best-ever basketball experience.

"One question," James added. "Are you the same Bart we used to know?"

"Yeah, it's me," Bart said. "Me plus a few hundred hours spent this summer with my cousin in Tulsa. He played on a Tulsa U. basketball team a long time ago. He was a playmaker, and he put me through some drills. And more drills. It was hard work, but like he says, *Skills are good, but nothing beats hard work.*"

I nodded. "Sounds like something Coach Robison would say."

At that moment Coach Robison stepped from his office. He didn't blow his whistle. He clapped his hands to get our attention.

"Great news, men," he said. "We will play our game tomorrow as scheduled against the Wolfhounds from the Midwest Region. The remaining Achukmas will arrive early tomorrow afternoon. So, it's home for our locals, and the van is waiting to take some of you to your motel rooms. I will see you there tonight for supper."

"Great news!" I shouted.

As Coach turned to leave, I pulled on his sleeve. Being the Choctaw mind reader that he was, he tilted his head, telling me to follow him to his office. He shut the door and leaned against his desk.

"Bobby, you must not tell anyone what I'm about to say. Not even Faye."

"I promise, Coach. Is Johnny hoke?"

"Not only is he hoke," Coach said, "but he will play in the game tomorrow."

"What! Is it safe?"

"It will be," he said, "and badman Billy will be sent back where he belongs."

"To prison?" I asked.

"For a long time," Coach replied.

CHAPTER 13

Danger Wears a Dark Hat

Unbelievable as it may sound, the evening and next morning went by with no surprises.

Dad dropped me off at the gym, and the parking lot was already filling up with fans, both ours and the Wolfhounds'. I hurried to the dressing room, but I wasn't the first Achukma. Johnny, already dressed and ready to play, stood up and greeted me.

"Halito," he said, *hello* in Choctaw.

"Cherokee Johnny! Great to see you!"

"Great to be here," said Johnny.

We were soon surrounded by Achukma teammates. Coach Robison stepped from his office and clapped his hands.

"Warm-up time, men! Layups, jump shots, and free throws. You all know the drill. Let's go!"

We dashed to the court and were soon sweating and ready to play. With warm-ups over and the game about to start, we gathered in a circle around Coach Robison. Instead of giving us an inspirational speech, Coach looked nervously at the scorer's table. I glanced that way, and there stood Detective Hancock, talking to the referees.

What is going on? I asked myself.

I looked at Johnny and he shrugged his shoulders. We soon had our answer. The head referee motioned for Coach to join the discussion, and when Coach returned, he spoke in a quiet but very serious voice.

"Say not a word, but follow me," he said. As he led us to the dressing room, I looked over my shoulder and saw the Wolfhounds also retreating to their dressing room. From the bleachers on both sides of the gym, the fans cheered their teams as they passed by, both the Achukmas and the Wolfhounds. The announcer's voice soon boomed over the cheers, and the crowd grew silent.

"We have a short break. In fifteen minutes, the teams will return to the court and the game will begin."

Coach walked quickly and, without hesitating, led us through the back door of the gym to the janitor's storage room, a small brick building beside the gym. He unlocked the door and motioned for us to enter.

"This is for your safety, men. Billy, the man who attacked Johnny's family, has been spotted in the parking lot. He has no idea we know what he looks like," Coach said. "We've got to keep it that way."

I looked at Johnny and watched as he closed his eyes and slowly nodded. We were all afraid for him, but what was he thinking? Johnny was always the most confident player on our team—not bragging and boastful, but quietly confident that he could get the rebound, make the shot, and keep his man from scoring. And he was always right. Almost always.

Now Johnny was afraid.

I scooted over next to him and wrapped my arm around his shoulders. "We've lived through worse," I whispered. He opened his eyes wide and shook his head in reply. I took a deep breath and realized that he was right.

I had lived through worse, when I smashed my car through the fence and drove into the lake, almost drowning. But we had never seen anything this crazy, this bad. A criminal stalking Cherokee Johnny and his family, and maybe even his basketball teammates.

A soft knock on the door made me jump and brought me back to the present. Coach stepped outside. When he returned after only a minute, he closed the door behind him and looked every one of us in the eyes, with a big smile on his face. "We've got a plan," he said, "and I like it. We still get to play our game tonight."

"All right."

"Yeah!"

"That's a relief."

"No way!"

"I'm liking it."

Everyone spoke or nodded or both, and we all breathed a huge sigh of relief, as if all the world's problems were now solved. After another minute, Johnny asked, "Can you tell us the plan, Coach?" His voice had little confidence.

"Sure thing, Johnny," said Coach. "Detective Hancock has assembled a group of plainclothes policemen, and they will be sitting in the stands, cheering us on. And here's the key. There's a sign posted outside the entrance to the gym. It says: *All attendees must go through a security check before entering the gymnasium.*"

"What does that mean?" I asked.

"It is a tight security check, Bobby. Like at an airport. Billy is out in the parking lot now, about to come inside. When he does, he will have to empty his pockets and step through a metal detector."

"A metal detector!" we all hollered.

"Yes," said Coach, "just like at the airport. We expect Billy to see what's happening and return to his car. If he has a gun or a knife, even a pocketknife, he'll have to leave them behind."

"Do you think he will still come into the gym?" Johnny asked.

"If he does, we're ready for him. He will be surrounded by plainclothes policemen, men who appear to be regular fans. But they will make certain Billy does not cause anyone harm or in any way disturb the game."

"And if he drives away?" I asked.

"If he drives away, we have two police cars waiting to pull him over and check his car for weapons," Coach Robison said. "If a gun is found, he can go back to prison for a parole violation, plus face charges for what he has done."

"Wow," I said. "Sounds like you've got all the bases covered."

"Let's get up! Stretch your legs and follow me to the gym like we've got all the bases covered for a big win tonight!" Coach said in an almost holler.

And we did. We climbed the steps of the janitor's closet, ducked through the door, and trotted after Coach. In a big hurry now, we dashed through the back door of the dressing room and, waving our arms high, flashed onto the court. We were soon joined by the Wolfhounds, and the crowd exploded.

"It's about time!" shouted somebody's dad.

Fans and classmates stood and clapped and cheered to see us and the Wolfhounds, ready to play.

"Nice to get back to reality, huh, Johnny?" I said and laughed.

"Feels like we've been time travelling," he replied, "to a future I can do without."

We hurried to the bench, with the subs sitting down and the starters surrounding Coach. "Now, men," he said, "I'm going to say b-ball time, and Bobby will count to four, and I want everybody shouting it so loud the roof will rattle. Understood?"

We all nodded in total agreement. Now it was basketball time. Nothing else.

"B-ball time," Coach whispered, and as if everyone in the gymnasium understood, a silence settled like a cloud.

"One, two, three, four," I whispered.

"B-ball time!" we shouted.

The cheerleaders picked up the chant, and the stands rocked with

> "B-ball time,
> B-ball time,
> Go, Achukmas,
> B-ball time!"

The ref tossed up the ball and Johnny got the tip. I grabbed the ball from the outstretched arms of a Wolfhound and threw it to Creek Eddie, who took two quick dribbles. He stopped near the baseline, pivoted with his back to the basket, and threw me a pass chest-high. I caught the ball and held it over my head, waiting for Johnny to settle in at the high post.

I faked a pass and my defender took a step back. Our many fans knew me. They knew what was about to happen. I couldn't let them down.

I launched a three-pointer as the crowd sucked in their collective breath, "AHHHhhhh."

Sweet music to my ears, I thought, as the ball nestled at the bottom of the net!

Achukmas 3

Wolfhounds 0

It didn't take long for us to learn that the Wolfhounds didn't play the usual "toss it in to the big man" game. Maybe six seconds, maybe seven. Their six-foot ten-inch post man outsprinted everyone to the other end of the court, caught a long pass, and dunked the ball.

Achukmas 3

Wolfhounds 2

"Wake up!" Coach shouted. I shook my head, ashamed, as I caught the inbounds pass and dribbled downcourt. As soon as I crossed midcourt, my defender ran at me hard. I turned my back to him, dribbling with my left hand. He didn't stop! He bumped me hard and no foul was called. I stumbled but didn't lose my dribble.

"Ref!" Coach shouted. "How could you miss that?"

The referees, of course, ignored him as play continued. Johnny ran from the baseline to the high post, and I tossed him the ball. He read my mind and knew that I wanted it back. With a defender that aggressive, I might score again.

I caught the ball and faked hard to my right, as I always did, then swirled around to the left. My defender was ready, and he dove for the ball, pushing me aside. I was ready too. I switched back to my right and left him behind, driving to the basket. I faked a pass to Mato and sank a layup.

As I turned to run upcourt, at full speed with all five Achukmas, my man stuck out his leg and almost tripped me.

"I hope you try that again," he said with a sneer.

I soon learned that he was their toughest defender, and not a star scorer. No, that was left up to their big men, all three big men, all over six feet seven inches tall. They were giants for high school basketball, at least where we came from. Johnny and Mato tried playing in front of them and preventing the pass, but the guards just lobbed the ball over their heads for easy buckets.

After three straight inside baskets by the Wolfhounds, Coach called a time-out.

"Men, let's fall back into a zone defense. Bobby and Eddie, when your man doesn't have the ball, fall back in the post and help out. We'll see if their guards can score. Now, let's go!"

A usual, Coach Robison knew what he was doing. When Eddie's man had the ball in the corner, and mine was across court, I fell back to help Mato and Johnny guard the big Wolfhounds. Sometimes it worked and sometimes it didn't.

When a big man caught the ball and took a dribble before jumping to the basket, I was there to steal the ball and speed downcourt. If the big man simply caught the ball and turned to the basket, he could jump over Johnny for a bank-shot basket. At least we kept the game within reach at halftime.

Achukmas 30

Wolfhounds 35

As we gathered on the dressing room benches for Coach Robison's halftime speech, Detective Hancock stepped through the door.

"Coach," he said, motioning with his finger, "let's talk, just for a minute."

When Coach returned, he shook his head and sighed. "Billy has disappeared," he said. "He parked his truck outside, and the policemen were about to arrest him. Then a busload of Wolfhound fans pulled up between him and the patrol car.

When the bus pulled away, Billy was gone. His truck is still here, but he's gone."

"Did he come into the gym?" I asked.

"They had security at the door, and no one saw him."

"Coach," Johnny said, "I am not afraid. I am here to play basketball."

"And we are here to win this game," Coach replied. "Now, I think we saw their big men can dribble and pass and break our full-court press. They've been doing it all year. But not for an entire game. Men, I want us to start the game by dropping back in your usual half-court, man-to-man defense. For the first minute or two. When you hear me holler *Now men, now*! It's time to press.

"We want to surprise them with the press and get a quick steal and basket. Then keep up the press till they start to tire and throw the ball away. We can win this, Achukmas."

"Yes!" we shouted, and we joined hands in a tight circle.

"One, two, three, four," I whispered.

"B-ball time!" we once again shouted.

The Wolfhounds won the second half tip-off, as expected. As soon as my "toughman," my defender, caught the ball, Eddie and I were all over him, waving our hands and making it hard for him to pass.

"Oh," he said, "something new. Let's see how you like this." He lowered himself, then rose up quickly, bashing my jaw with his elbow. I fell to the floor.

"Sorry," he said, stepping over me and dribbling away. But not for long.

WWWWWrrrrrrrr! WWWWWrrrrrrrr! The nearest referee blew his whistle.

"Foul!" he shouted. "Flagrant foul!"

"No way! He was in my face! You can't call a foul on me!" Toughman shouted.

"You had better back away and shut up," the referee said in a serious tone. "You are lucky to still be here, with your first-half fouls. We have seen enough."

"No! I was protecting myself!" he said, knowing he was lying as I rolled to my knees and stood up. The crowd of Achukma fans booed loudly, and Coach Robison ran to help me. He helped me to the bench and called for our team doctor to check me out.

"Can you see out of both eyes?" he asked.

"Yes, and I'll be fine. Except for a bruise, I'm hoke," I said, doing my best to be allowed to play.

"Let's go to the dressing room, Bobby. For a few minutes, just to be sure."

I stood up tall and took a few quick jumps before I followed him to the dressing room. As soon as we entered, he shut the door, saying, "Just a few simple drills, Bobby. Lift your right arm. Now touch your left ear. Now bend over and straighten up slowly."

After a few minutes of drills, he said, "I'm allowing you to play, Bobby. Avoid those elbows and good luck!"

As soon as I stepped to the court, a slow cheer rose from the crowd, and soon our Achukma fans were on their feet, clapping and cheering. I looked to the Wolfhound bench, and Toughman was nowhere to be seen. "He's gone, Bobby," Coach Robison said, reading my mind. "He kept hollering till the referees threw him out."

"Glad to hear that," I said, sitting on the bench. "So, maybe I can play?"

Coach patted me on the knee. "Soon, Bobby. Soon," he said.

Eddie hit a baseline jump shot, and I glanced at the scoreboard.

Achukmas 39

Wolfhounds 43

Everyone sprinted back on defense, then set up our full-court press. Eddie took a step away when his man caught the inbounds pass, but as soon as he took a dribble, Eddie was there. He swiped the ball and drove in for a layup!

Achukmas 41

Wolfhounds 43

When a Wolfhound big man missed a short bank shot, Coach stood up and shouted, "Time out!" The referees blew their whistles.

"Bobby, check in," he said, and I hurried to the scorer's table. When I returned to the bench, Coach had that winning look on his face.

"Let's stay with the press," he said. "It's working often enough. And we'll add one thing to our offense that will win this game."

We all looked at each other as our confidence grew.

"Are you ready, Bobby?" Coach asked. "With your cheek bruised, it won't be safe for you to drive to the bucket. Maybe you can nail a few three-pointers?"

All eyes were on me. What could I say?

"I'm ready," I said. "Let's do it!"

I tossed the ball inbounds to Eddie, who threw it to Mato, standing on the free-throw line with his back to the basket. He spun around, took a single dribble, then tossed the ball over his shoulder. He knew exactly where I would be waiting, at the top of the key. I caught the ball, took a dribble and a step back, and launched a high, soft jumper. Nothing but net!

Achukmas 44

Wolfhounds 43

We traded baskets for the remainder of the third quarter. We went for the steal, and if we got it, we had a clear shot. If not, their big men had an easy shot near the basket.

I hit two more three-pointers, and at the end of the quarter we were down by two.

Achukmas 49

Wolfhounds 51

"Stay with the press, and turn up the speed on offense," Coach said. "They are not used to running an entire game, and it will catch up with those big men, Speed and smarts will win."

The Wolfhounds brought their big men downcourt to help with the press, and it worked for a while. They caught the inbounds passes and handed off to guards running by. But Coach was right. They soon began breathing hard and slowing down.

With two minutes to go in the game, and the Wolfhounds up by three, they had the ball. Mato was guarding his man close to the basket, and when a pass sailed inside, he stepped in front of his man and swatted the ball away. Johnny picked it up, tossed me a pass to midcourt, and I fed Eddie for a layup.

Achukmas 65

Wolfhounds 66

The Wolfhound coach called for a time-out. By now every fan in the bleachers was on their feet, stomping and clapping and shouting "Achukmas" from one side of the court and "Wolfhounds" from the other.

"Have a seat, men," Coach Robison said. "You are all so eager to win, to do anything to win. And you will. But you need to put your minds to work, to play smart."

He then looked around our circle, meeting eyes with every Achukma. "You know where the ball is going, Mato. Inside. To your man. And you know which way your man will turn to shoot. Overplay your man so hard to that side, he'll have to turn the other way. And when he does, Creek Eddie will be there. Right, Eddie?"

Eddie lifted his head and stared at Coach. Coach Robison had never called him Creek Eddie. His teammates did, but not Coach. First Eddie smiled. Then he laughed, softly at first. When he saw us all staring at him, he greeted us with a loud belly laugh.

"Yes, sir, I'll be there," Eddie said, still laughing.

Coach knew how to make us relax.

When the referee blew his whistle and the game started again, it all played out as Coach predicted. Eddie was there, waiting for the ball when the big man turned. He made the steal, threw me the ball, and as I drove for the basket, a Wolfhound dove for the ball and hit me instead. No pain, but the referee blew his whistle.

"Foul, two shots!" he shouted.

With the game on the line, I stepped to the free-throw line, with five seconds left on the clock. One make and we were tied. Two makes and we had a great chance to win. I dribbled the ball as the entire gym fell silent. Everyone was holding their breath. Suddenly, Dad shouted at the top of his voice.

"Bobby!"

I looked to the bleachers where Dad was standing. Everyone, thousands of spectators and fans, all looked at Dad. I knew what they were thinking: *What is that crazy man doing?*

They didn't know he was my dad. They all thought he was trying to make me miss the free throws. The policemen stood up and started shoving their way through the crowd in Dad's direction—to arrest him!

"In the days of my youth!" Dad hollered.

That's the song that was playing when I drove the car into Lake Thunderbird, almost killing myself! Dad was trying to tell me something. But what?

Dad leaned to one side and pointed behind himself, where a big man with a huge black cowboy hat sat. The man was pulling the hat over his face, and right away I knew who it was. It was Billy, and that's why he snuck in undetected.

I had to do something. I stepped away from the free-throw line, pulled back my right arm, and threw the longest, hardest basketball pass of my life, right at Dad. He nodded his head up and down as the crowd cheered, thinking I was firing at him.

Nope. Just before the basketball hit Dad, he ducked down. The ball smacked Billy in the head, knocking his hat off. The cops were already close, and when they saw Billy, the man they were looking to arrest, they grabbed him. One cop blew his whistle and waved his arms, shouting, "Move away, we're coming through!"

The fans, still totally confused, gave them a path to the floor, and soon Billy was hauled away, out the door, and into a waiting police car. The referees approached the scorer's table and called for a brief time-out.

"Coaches and players, stay where you are!" one referee shouted. As soon as everyone was settled into their seats, he blew his whistle.

"Play on," he said, and he handed me the basketball as if nothing had happened.

I once again took a few dribbles and a deep breath. I balanced the ball on my right palm and lifted a high-arching shot, which hit only net.

Achukma fans cheered, then stopped and fell silent as the ref handed me the ball again. I closed my eyes, lifted my head, and then opened my eyes again. A smile crossed my face as free-throw number two split the cords. I jumped high and waved my fists to the sky!

"Not yet!" Coach shouted.

As soon as I landed, a Wolfhound player grabbed the ball and stepped out of bounds. His fastest big man was running downcourt. The crowd moaned as the big man caught a long pass and stepped to the basket.

"He'll win the game with a dunk!" I shouted. "No!"

No was right. Didn't happen. Cherokee Johnny anticipated the play. He leapt behind the Wolfhound and swatted the dunk shot away, just as the buzzer sounded.

Achukmas 67

Wolfhound 66

CHAPTER 14

Post-Game News

Following a night of after-game celebration at the gym, with catered pizza and hamburgers and ice-cold drinks for the Achukmas and their parents, we drove home and crashed out. Sometime around nine the next morning, the doorbell rang. I jumped out of bed as Dad answered the door. He and Mom welcomed Detective Hancock into the living room.

"There has been a new development you need to be aware of," he said. "Billy, as you know, was captured at the basketball game last night."

Out of respect for Detective Hancock, I didn't interrupt him. I just raised my hand and waved it back and forth. I had to know. He took a long breath, lifted his eyebrows, and looked to Dad, as if to say, *How do you live with him?*

Dad just smiled.

"Do you have a question, Bobby?" asked Detective Hancock.

"Yes, thank you," I said. "How did Billy get past security?"

"I hate to admit it," he said, "but we missed him. When the bus pulled in front of the gym with the Wolfhound fans, he must have jumped out of his truck and joined them. They had several fathers of players who were tall, like Billy, so he fit right in. He wore that cowboy hat pulled down over his face and a shirt the color of their bright red jerseys, so he did his research.

"But we have him now. He has been arrested for causing the injury to Mr. Mackey and for tossing the firebomb through the Mackeys' window."

"What is his motive?" Dad asked. "Did Mackey help convict him of a crime?"

"That is the biggest surprise of all," Hancock replied. "And that is why the information provided by your son, Bobby, and his friend Faye was so valuable. Without it, we would never have suspected Billy of these crimes.

"He was convicted of armed robbery, and tried and sentenced in another county a hundred miles from here. But his cellmate, Tony Herald, was prosecuted by Mr. Mackey. He was recently released on good behavior after serving ten years of a maximum twenty-year sentence."

I had to ask. "Did Tony have anything to do with this? He had more reason than Billy to be angry at Johnny's dad."

"Bobby, do you recall why you asked Willie for his card? Why you conned your way to the picnic table with Willie and his team of parolees?" Hancock glanced at Dad, saying, "Excuse my use of the word *conned*, but you know your son better than I do."

"Yes, I do," Dad said as he and the detective shared an *almost* invisible smile.

"Of course, I remember," I said. "Billy was a bully and had to be warned by Willie not to hurt anyone. And a fellow parolee made a joke about Billy knowing how to use a ladder. That was only two days after Mr. Mackey's injury on the broken ladder."

"You are correct," Hancock said. "You spotted his bullying ways. Our theory is that with his former cellmate free, he would give Tony the gift of revenge—break the hip of his prosecuting attorney."

"What! Was that why he hurt Johnny's dad?" I asked. "To deliver what you call the gift of revenge?"

"I am afraid so."

"Does Tony Herald know?" I asked. "Is he part of the plan?"

"We have picked up Tony, and his parole officer is meeting us at the station in an hour," Detective Hancock said. "Since he was Billy's cellmate and has a motive, we are required to question him."

"Will you please keep us informed?" Dad asked.

"And do you think Billy is alone in going after Johnny's family?" I asked. "So, you're thinking he was in the backyard and threw the firebomb?"

"Bobby, we did install a backyard camera, motion-sensitive," Hancock said. "We saw Billy's car pass by the Mackeys' residence a short while before the firebomb. But he did not enter the backyard."

"Then how…?" I asked.

"We will find that out during our interrogation," Detective Hancock answered. "We did see the firebomb sail over the fence and through the kitchen window. But nothing else."

"Johnny is a hero whether he admits it or not," I said.

Everyone in the room, even Detective Hancock, nodded *yes*.

"And here's some good news," Hancock added. "I believe that Tony Herald became a different man during his ten-year prison stay. We will find out more as we question him, but I think he's a changed man."

"Let's hope so," Mom said.

Detective Hancock rose from his chair and walked to the door. "The officer will remain here for now, with his patrol car in your driveway as a warning," he said. "We have no reason to believe you are in any danger now that Billy is in custody, but we will take no chances. You have been very helpful."

With that friendly farewell, he tipped his hat and turned to go.

"Oh! Just a minute," Mom said, leaping from her chair. "I baked an apple pie last night. Let me cut you a piece, Detective."

"Thank you, but I should be going," he said. Then he saw the disappointment on Mom's face. "Well, all right, if you insist," he said with a smile. "Can you box it up and I'll take it with me?"

Mom soon returned with a box big enough to carry the whole pie. "I cut a few extra pieces for your family," she said, shrugging her shoulders and laughing.

"Bobby," Hancock said, "you are one lucky young man."

"So is Bobby's dad," said Dad, as we both shared memories of the flaky crust and drippingly delicious apple pie now walking out the door!

Twenty minutes later the phone rang and Dad answered it.

"Sure," Dad said. "We'll be there as soon as we can. Twenty minutes?"

He hung up the phone and closed his eyes. When he reopened them, a slight smile crossed his face. "We need to join Coach Robison and parolee Tony at the police station," he said.

"Now?" Mom asked. "Did I hear that right?"

"Yes, and I'll explain as we drive. Let's go!"

We hurried to the car, and I felt a rush of powerful emotions. Nothing bad had happened or Dad would have told us.

We are about to witness a miracle, I thought. *I know it.*

CHAPTER 15

Forgiveness in a Bag

As we entered the station, Detective Hancock greeted us and led us to an interrogation room. There sat Tony, Coach Robison, and Cherokee Johnny, together with his mom and dad. Beside them sat Lloyd and his mom and dad.

"Thank you for coming," Coach said.

"I asked you all to be here," said Tony. "Without Bobby and Lloyd, I would be back in prison."

"We can now proceed," said Detective Hancock, pointing to Tony.

"I know this has been a fearful time for all of you." Tony said. "I meant no harm to any of you. Mr. Mackey, I never blamed you for what

I did. And I have learned so much over the past ten years. Prison does that."

He lifted his eyes and looked quietly at each of us. "I will be moving away," he said, "so you won't have to worry about me anymore."

I watched as Johnny gave a quiet sigh of relief.

"But I want to leave you a gift," Tony said, "with the permission of Detective Hancock."

"Permission already granted," Hancock said with a smile.

Tony lifted a large paper bag and plopped it on the table—and out rolled a basketball! "Willie gave it to me," he said, "and I knew right away that you young men deserved it more than I did."

"Let's let Johnny have it!" I shouted.

"Johnny has climbed the tallest mountain for the past few weeks," Coach Robison said. "I think he does deserve your gift. Your very thoughtful gift, Tony."

"We're finally all back," I said. "We are one big basketball family!"

"We have climbed the highest mountain," Dad said.

"And what name would you give this mountain we've climbed?" Coach asked.

No one spoke as everyone cast their eyes around the table. Of course, somebody had to break the silence. "I think Johnny should name the mountain," I said. "He's climbed the steepest mountain of all."

Johnny gave me that sly smile and took a breath. He closed his eyes and bowed his head in thought. When he lifted his head and opened his eyes, we saw the Johnny we knew, strong and confident—and caring.

"We have just climbed the mountain of justice," he said. "Justice Mountain. Justice for all. And for you especially, Tony."

We lifted our glasses high, and everyone said in unison,

"Justice for all."

About the Author

Tim Tingle is an Oklahoma Choctaw and an award-winning author and storyteller. Tingle performs a Choctaw story before Chief Batton's State of the Nation Address at every Choctaw Nation Labor Day Festival.

In June 2011, Tingle spoke at the Library of Congress and performed at the Kennedy Center in Washington, DC. From 2011 to 2016, he was featured at Choctaw Days, a celebration at the Smithsonian's National Museum of the American Indian.

Tingle's great-great-grandfather, John Carnes, walked the Trail of Tears in 1835. In 1992, Tim retraced the trail to Choctaw homelands in Mississippi, a journey that inspired his first book, *Walking the Choctaw Road*. Tim's first Pathfinders novel, *Danny Blackgoat: Navajo Prisoner*, was an American Indian Youth Literature Awards Honor Book in 2014.

In 2018, Tingle received the Arrell Gibson Lifetime Achievement Award from the Oklahoma Center for the Book. That same year, *A Name Earned*, the third book in his No Name series for young readers, earned a Kirkus starred review.

PathFinders novels offer exciting contemporary and historical stories featuring Native teens and written by Native authors. For more information, visit: NativeVoicesBooks.com

Tim Tingle's No Name series tells the story of Bobby Byington, a Choctaw teen who is proud to be a starter on his high school basketball team but whose personal life is filled with turmoil. Basketball and friendship are driving forces as Bobby and his friends deal with parental alcoholism, school bullies, and prejudice.

No Name
978-1-93905-306-0 • $9.95

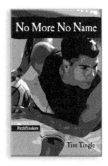

No More No Name
978-1-93905-317-6 • $9.95

A Name Earned
978-1-939053-18-3 • $9.95

Trust Your Name
978-1-939053-19-0 • $9.95